Snowed In on Valentine's Day

Alana Highbury

Content Note

This book contains the following content.

If you'd rather avoid any spoilers, skip this page!

Explicit scenes: None.
Language: Mild swearing.
Themes: Mental health issues, occasional alcohol consumption.

Dearest Mr. Highbury,
It's your turn

Chapter 1

I love weddings.

I adore them, actually.

I love *this* wedding. I love my best friend like a sister. And I've even grown to like Mariana's fiancé, Terry, though I still preferred to call him Mr. Pinecone. Probably because I'll never forget the ridiculous costume he was wearing when we met.

I mean, her *husband*. Mariana was no longer engaged. She was married. Wedded. Stuck with Terry forever.

But as she took a sip of champagne and flashed a brilliant smile at the love of her life, I knew that "stuck" was the furthest thing from her mind. She'd never looked more beautiful, and it wasn't only because of her shimmery white strapless dress or the sparkly yet classy jewels she wore. It was because she'd found the one. Between Mari and me, I'd always been the romantic, and she teased me about my obsession with rom-com movies and Valentine's Day.

But to see her now … she was happy. Deliriously so.

And I … well, I was happy for her—*happy* my best friend was finally living her life with joy and love and all the things denied to her for so long. Happy she was married on Christmas Eve, her favorite day in the world.

I was happy for her. Truly.

But you're not happy.

I flinched at the unbidden thought and quickly downed the rest of my champagne.

I scanned the scene before us. The wedding party was

small, so it was just the four of us at the head table in the reception hall. However, the guests numbered in the hundreds. One would expect a highly private person like Mari to insist on a small wedding. But she wanted to invite all her staff at the resort, and Terry knew everyone in town, so basically everyone in our little town of Shipsvold was present. I made eye contact with Nora, who was not only Terry's grandmother but also one of my favorite people. She winked, and once again, I arranged my features in what I hoped was a genuine smile before my eyes continued sweeping the cavernous room.

Still, it was lonely up here. And I was thirsty.

"Hey, Mari," I said while patting her bare shoulder gently. "I'll be right back, OK?"

With her hand still holding Terry's on the table, she turned her head toward me, offering a wide smile that slid right off her face when she eyed me. "Is everything OK, Haz?"

Since when was Mari so good at reading people? Maybe she had always been good at this. I was usually easy to read. Usually happy. Laid back. Taking life a day at a time. That's me. Easygoing Hazel.

But I only laughed. "It's not OK. It's *wonderful*. I'm just thirsty."

Her eyebrows rose ever so slightly, and she stared into my eyes for a moment. "All right," she said slowly, watching as I placed my napkin on the table and stood up.

I gave her a wide smile before turning toward the bar, and my face fell.

Ugh, not that guy.

Standing at the bar was the impeccably groomed—and, I have to admit, *hot* by any standards—man I'd walked down the aisle with earlier today. I'd been introduced to Peter Auclair last night when he flew in for the wedding rehearsal, but he'd not spoken a word to me after that initial "Nice to meet you, Ms. Tanaka-Katz." My nervous chatter and laughs just before the ceremony were met with a tight jaw and a blank stare. I even felt his biceps tense up when we linked arms down the aisle.

I sauntered up to the bar and pulled out the bar stool nearest to him. After carefully arranging the flowy layers of my pale green bridesmaid dress in front of me, I sat down. He stilled but didn't turn to look at me.

"What can I get you, ma'am?"

I tried not to glare at the barely-legal kid who just ma'am-ed me. Was he even old enough to tend bar? "Uh, yeah, I'd like some more champ—actually, you know what? I'd like a shot. Maybe a few. Do you have any of those fruit-flavored vodkas?"

The kid nodded, pointing behind him to his left. I scanned the shelf. "Oh, is that purple one grape? I want that."

"Purple vodka, coming right up," he said, spinning around to make my shot.

I stole a glance at the silent man next to me and opened my mouth to speak, but then the kid was back already with a shot glass of my favorite drink.

I downed it quickly and pointed at the empty glass before looking at the boy. "Keep them coming, please."

The kid gave me a side-eye glance but poured another.

I decided to just sip this one. Yes, drunken oblivion sounded appealing right about now, but I doubt Mari would be happy if I returned to her table smashed.

I moaned, loving the sweetness on my tongue. "Just what I needed."

Peter finally looked over at me then, but only briefly, his lips tight and eyes revealing nothing.

Screw this. "Um, hello?" Facing him, I took another sip.

A lengthy sigh escaped his mouth as he turned toward me, still leaning against the bar. "Hello," he said in his deep baritone.

"Do you remember me? I'm—"

"I do."

I cracked a real smile. "We're not getting married, man. I'm just saying hello."

His brows were furrowed as he opened his mouth to speak, but no words came for a long moment. Finally, his mask of indifference returned. "Excuse me?"

My smile faltered. "You said, 'I do'—you know, like in a wedding ..." I trailed off, seeing that he didn't find this amusing at all. It was funny, wasn't it? Or was I already drunk? "Never mind."

He said nothing but held eye contact for a long time. Finally, he spoke again. "Can I help you with something—"

I put my hands up in the universal symbol for *stop* as I winced. "Please don't ma'am me. Once was enough. My vanity is already crushed. I'm not even thirty yet, or at least not until New Year's Eve. Yeah, would you believe I was born on that day, of all days? But I didn't even get the honor of being the last baby born in the hospital that day. It was some jerk named Preston." I shook my head. "Can you believe it?"

His brows furrowed again, but only for a split second. "I do believe you just called a *baby* a jerk."

"Well, he was! I mean, with a name like Preston, he has to be, right?"

His face was devoid of expression as he shook his head. "If you say so."

"Well, I do." I giggled. "There, now I did it too. I said, 'I do.' Well, good thing that boy over there's just a bartender and not an ordained minister. Or else you'd have just found yourself married to this hot mess." I waved my hand up and down once with a self-deprecating smile.

"I don't think that's how it works."

I stared ahead at the gleaming countertop. "So, you want to know why I'm a hot mess?" I didn't turn to look, afraid he'd be shaking his head no. Because I needed to vent. He was probably the worst choice in terms of people to vent to, but, well, he was here. Alone, just like me. Well, presumably alone. I didn't see anyone with him earlier, and he wasn't wearing a wedding band.

"Well, where do I even begin?" I sighed. "My best friend— my only close friend, really—just got married today, and don't get me wrong ... it was a beautiful ceremony, and she was gorgeous. I'm super happy for her, but I'm going to miss the two-single-ladies thing we had going on. Well, maybe we never had that going on exactly—she never liked to party. But anyway, yeah. Pinecone's a good guy. You know that, I guess, since you're his BFF. I didn't know that at first. You see, he had ghosted her like a decade ago, and when they met up again, he was kind of a jerk. No, not kind of. He was awful. But it turns out he *didn't* ghost her, and his evil sister—you know what, never mind. That part's not important." I paused, taking a sip of the newly filled shot placed in front of me. Then I narrowed my eyes while scanning his face. "Or wait, maybe you knew all that? You guys are close, I suppose."

His nod was barely perceptible, but I took it as fuel to keep going.

"But I'm happy for them because I'm all about romance, happily ever afters—there's not a rom-com you could name that I wouldn't have seen already." I bit my lip to keep from laughing. "But you probably can't name a lot of rom-coms, can you, Pete? You're not that kind of guy." I downed the rest of the shot and waved at the bartender again.

"It's Peter."

"What—oh. Not Pete. Got it. That's too bad, as I like the name Pete." It was my maternal grandfather's name, after all. He was my favorite person, and he'd died when I was in high school. I felt my throat get tight while thinking of the only grandfather I'd ever known. The best one a girl could have. Well, I met my Japanese grandfather as a toddler, but I can't muster any memory of it. Dad said it was probably for the best. I sighed, thinking of how much I missed my family this year.

"Do you have family you usually celebrate Christmas with?" I looked at him closely, but he only shook his head quickly. "Ah, that's … well, I guess it's sad for most people, but you don't look sad." I thought I detected a tightening of his jaw then, but it came and went so fast that I couldn't be sure. "Well, I usually *do* see my family, but this year I can't. Do you want to know why?" I didn't wait for an answer, knowing he likely wouldn't give one anyway. "Because *I'm* always visiting *them*. I always travel to see my mom in Paris or wherever she is, or I go to Japan to see Dad, sometimes my sister. The *one time* I couldn't travel, I hoped they'd come visit. But did they? Nope."

Tears pooled in my eyes, and I willed them to not fall. I never trusted waterproof mascara. "It's fine. I mean, it sucks. But I'm used to it. Used to being alone. So it's weird, right? I'm the biggest romantic I know. Like, Valentine's Day is one of my favorite holidays; I'm basically in love with love. Yet my love life is so bad. Either the dates are bad, or the relationships don't last long. Don't get me wrong, I date a lot. *A lot.* But I can't find someone who—" I stopped, seeing his face. This time his jaw definitely tightened, and the muscle in his cheek contracted. "OK, I'll stop. I don't mind being single that much, but it's harder around the holidays, you know?" I eyed him again. He probably *didn't* know. A guy that attractive would have an active dating life *if* he wasn't already in a serious relationship. My throat tightened as I considered that. What if he was?

Beyond awkward, that's what.

Change the subject, Hazel.

I flipped my hair over my shoulder. I'd planned to wear an updo, but Mari had reminded me my long, silky black hair was one of my best assets, so I went with a natural look. "I don't know why I'm telling you this because I haven't told anyone else yet, but ... I need to change careers. I'm tired of doing what I'm doing. Tired of ... being tired. From work. From the emotional labor I draw upon day in and day out as I travel around the country, sometimes around the world." I paused, frowning when I noticed my shot glass was still empty. "If they didn't tell you, I'm sort of a motivational speaker. I do a lot of events at Mari's resort, but I also travel and do events all over. I'm good at it, but ... I want something else. I want to spend more time writing, maybe helping people one on one. The constant travel ... well, let's just say I've had a lifetime of it already, and it's enough. I can't believe I'm saying this, but I want to settle down. Stay in one place. Maybe? It's such a foreign idea to me. I spent so many years—"

He cleared his throat, and I gazed at him in confusion.

I'd almost forgotten he was there.

"Sorry, was I rambling?" I laughed nervously. "I tend to do that. At least when I've had alcohol." I sighed, seeing no response on his beautiful face. "That's probably something I should change too. No more drinking."

He raised one eyebrow then, the most expressive thing I'd seen from him so far.

"I mean, after tonight. Or … maybe after New Year's Eve? Yes, it'll be my New Year's resolution. And then changing jobs."

I bit my lip, considering another idea. "Maybe I'll take a break from dating too. Or is that too many resolutions? It's hard to make a lot of changes at once." I looked at him for an answer, for some reason, though I knew he wouldn't supply one. "Well, why not? Doesn't hurt to try, does it?" I offered a small smile.

After a long moment of silence, his deep voice rumbled out of his chest, as though he rarely used it. "Are you done?"

I blinked a few times quickly. Am I *done*? Was he really asking me—

One look at his frown, and I knew. He wanted me to shut up.

And in the morning, I'd wish I had.

Chapter 2

"Hazel," came a muffled whisper.

Still muffled, the voice became louder and more insistent. "Haz, wake up …"

As awareness crept into my mind unwelcome, I groaned, burying my face into the fluffy pillow.

This can't be happening. Not again.

My head was going to explode, and my throat felt like Death Valley. And I was pretty sure some random guy's eyes would soon be meeting mine, just inches away. As soon as I could lift my head to see …

But no. Better to feign suffocation via pillow, I think. Maybe he'll take the hint and leave.

"Hazel Rei!" came a booming voice as he shook my shoulders. "*Wake up!*"

I tried to lift my head, but the stabbing pain kept it firmly on the pillow. Instead, I managed to turn it to the side, toward the voice. "Please, don't scream at me," I pleaded, still squeezing my eyes shut. "Just … you can just go now," I mumbled. But as more awareness seeped in, I realized the voice wasn't coming from the other side of the bed. And, wait, it wasn't very masculine. Plus, what were the odds I'd told some random guy my middle name?

I opened one eye slowly and then the other. Before I could fully register the look on *her* face, I snapped my eyes shut again. The pain, oh the pain.

"Hazel," Mariana said, this time not quite as loud. "You've

got to sit up. I've got the ibuprofen ready. Lots of water." When I didn't stir, she added, "And a coffee."

My eyes flew open then.

Coffee. Yes.

I tried to gather my strength and sit up. Wincing as my head pounded, I looked at my best friend as she sat next to me with a sympathetic smile.

"That bad, huh?" She handed me the painkiller capsules and water bottle.

I nodded and started chugging the water before grimacing.

"Woah, take it easy, Haz," said Mariana in a soothing yet loud voice. "You know you have to drink slowly when you're hung over."

"Ah—" I croaked. After a difficult swallow, I sipped some more water. Then she handed me the steaming mug, and I managed a smile. "Thanks."

"Listen, I wouldn't have bothered you, but it's 10 o'clock, and—" She paused, seeing my finger over my lips in a shushing expression. Not shouting this time, she continued, "We have one last brunch date before my trip. I couldn't miss this—"

"Your honeymoon! Not just a trip," I managed before taking several blissful sips of coffee. I sighed. "You're right. I'm going to miss you so much, lady." I tried to ignore the pounding in my skull with every word I spoke.

"I'll miss you too. Honestly, I'm nervous about leaving. I've never taken a vacation since owning the resort." Her usually smooth forehead was crinkled as she turned vulnerable eyes toward me. I was so proud of her. The Mari I'd known for most of our years of friendship had been so closed off emotionally, but she'd finally learned to share and experience her feelings—and *life*—more fully.

I reached over and squeezed her hand briefly. "You lovebirds are going to have an amazing time. And you deserve it after this crazy holiday season, am I right? With a *wedding* in the midst of it all!"

She nodded, her shoulder-length strawberry blond hair bouncing up and down. She was wearing her hair natural and wavy today, in contrast to the perfectly straightened blonde hair she'd carefully maintained for every waking second before she'd had an epiphany and reunited with Terry over a year ago. "The holiday season was intense, yeah. I think our first year running the Christmas village went well though. Jane told Terry she was proud of us. She'd never tell me herself though, of course," she said with a laugh as she sipped her tea. She was right though. Jane, who was married to Terry's grandmother, had previously owned the Christmas village—the heart of their town—until this year, but she liked to give Mariana a hard time.

"Never," I said with a smile.

Her eyes lit up as she looked at me again. "So, that New Year's party was pretty wild after we left, eh?"

I groaned. "Don't remind me. I'm a walking hangover. Everyone around for miles will know."

She shook her head. "Nah, they're all nursing their own headaches." She put her finger on her chin in a thoughtful manner. "Does Shipsvold have a drinking problem?"

"Well, yeah, that and every other town in the upper Midwest." I smiled wryly before my expression sobered. "But you know ... uh, I think I'm done."

"Done?" She raised her eyebrows, looking at my unfinished coffee. "With what?"

"Drinking." I sighed. "I am getting too old for this. I don't even like it that much anymore, honestly. It's definitely not worth feeling like this." I ran my finger over the rim of the cup. "I don't drink that often anyway. I just ... well, I'm thinking of making some life changes. Cutting out alcohol—or at least the heavy drinking—is one of the easier things."

Mari's eyes widened. "One of the easier ... what other changes? Please, please don't tell me you're moving away."

"Oh, hell no. The opposite actually. I want to stick around more. Sick of all the travel."

Her jaw dropped several inches, and then she took a

moment to form words. "You're—but the travel … I mean, it's your work. Your passion. Right?"

A flutter of something that felt, well, momentous rose within me. I took a deep, steadying breath. "Yes and no. My passion is helping people, convincing them they're worthy of love from themselves and others, helping women to see what they bring to the world. But traveling all over for speaking engagements is only one way to do that."

Her eyes were still wide. "Well, yes, that's true. It's just … I thought you were happy doing that. It was your dream."

I pressed my lips together before letting out a long breath. "I've been happy-*ish*. But it was never my dream. I kind of got swept away from all the attention years ago when my blog took off. And I would've done anything to escape the legal profession at that point, if you remember."

She nodded her head slowly. Of course she remembered, as I'd probably complained about being a lawyer every single day for the two years I practiced. Turns out I didn't hate law itself; I just hated the law practice I was in. Still, I suspected the culture was similar in most other law practices. When Mariana ended up purchasing the resort after an unexpected inheritance from a generous foster mom, I realized giving legal advice wasn't so bad. I was still good at it, and I could use that skill to help my best friend. Or family, I supposed. But Dad was the lawyer in the family, and even though he was retired and living in his native Japan now, everyone we knew still consulted him on everything, as though I didn't exist. So, I'd failed to impress not only my father but also pretty much all of my family and friends of the family. Sigh. It was never good to walk down that memory lane.

Mariana looked thoughtful for a long moment. "That all makes sense. But I suppose I thought you loved what you were doing. You never said otherwise."

I bit my lip. "You're right, I didn't. I wouldn't even say that I dislike it. I enjoy public speaking." I had to chuckle for a moment at Mariana's expression. She, like most people I'd met, loathed public speaking. Not me. "The energy at these events is

—well, you've seen it when you've hosted events at the resort. It's phenomenal and maybe addicting. I think … maybe I don't want to give it up entirely. I could do speaking engagements occasionally, especially if they're at the resort."

I drew in a deep breath. "And I need a break from the travel. I'm just over it."

"But you love traveling. I thought that was one of the perks of the job."

"For some people, yes." I looked down at my hands as I continued quietly, "But not for me."

Mariana was silent for a long time, and I finally looked up. In her eyes I saw understanding. Empathy. She nodded and offered a small smile. "Is that because you traveled so much as a child?"

"Yes, we traveled a lot, but we also moved around a lot. It's—" I stopped, feeling a lump in my throat. I inhaled slowly. "And then they moved away. All of them, one by one, to different corners of the earth. Dad seems content back in Japan, but Mom and Halley? They can't stay in one place for more than two years or so. I think … I'm different. I want to be different, that is. I like living in Shipsvold—staying in one place and putting down roots. You and now Pinecone … well, you're family too now."

My best friend nodded and squeezed my hand. "I feel the same. And it makes sense—you did buy a house. I mean, so did I. I'm sorry I was too distracted to realize what that meant for you."

"Well, it meant a lot for you too." I'd tried for years to convince her to buy or at least rent her own place. She'd been living in a large suite at the resort for as long as she'd owned it, and for a workaholic like Mari, it wasn't great for her. She finally decided to move out just over a year ago, and then Terry put his tree farm up for sale and moved into her lovely Victorian home.

"It was a big step for me, yes." The corners of her mouth turned down a bit. "Hazel, changing careers is a big deal. I mean, you know that. You've done it before. Can I ask … well, what will you do instead? Do you know?"

I chuckled before replying, "Of course you can ask. And I do know. I'm going to write more. And maybe even do one-on-one coaching or webinars, that sort of thing. It's great to talk to large groups, but the impact of helping someone one-on-one is unmatched. And it's just … it fits better with the quieter, more stable vibe I'm looking for right now."

She nodded. "I understand that. You know I'm the definition of introverted," she said with a slanted smile. "But you —"

"I know you're about to say I'm an extrovert. But I've been thinking I'm more of an ambivert." At her curious expression, I added, "Basically I fit somewhere in the middle of the scale—not an introvert but not an extrovert. If such a thing even exists. So, yeah, I want to do the same things and have the same goals but just in a different way."

Her head bobbed up and down. "You know, it fits. Everyone always compares you to Brene Brown or Geneen Roth, and I think they might spend more time writing books than holding in-person events. You can make it work." Her face morphed into a massive grin. "Wow, I'm so excited for you! This is huge." But her smile faded. "Wretched timing though. I'm leaving for my honeymoon tonight, or else I'd demand that we celebrate!"

I laughed. While most people's version of celebrating would mean a party or fancy dinner, Mari would probably invite approximately two people to her house for dinner and ice cream. And that was fine by me. I loved being around people, but I needed me time too. Right now, especially.

"While we're on the topic of New Year's goals, in addition to taking a break from alcohol and speaking tours, I have another resolution."

"Oh?" Her eyebrows rose, and she leaned forward.

My lips turned up at the corners. "No men."

"No—do you mean …" She paused and tilted her head thoughtfully. "Do you want to date women?"

I laughed. "No. I mean, maybe I shouldn't rule it out, but

that's not what I meant. I mean no dating anyone. I need a break, maybe a long one."

Her eyes were huge now as her mouth opened and then closed.

"You look shocked. Should I be offended? Am I a serial dater or something?" I asked her with a smile. When she didn't respond right away, my brows furrowed. "Wait, you think I am?"

"No!" She averted her eyes as I studied her expression.

"You totally do!"

She winced. "No, I—we wouldn't call it that, exactly."

I bit back a smile. "Oh, what would *we* call it then?"

"Well, we … um," she floundered as she took a nervous sip of her tea, now cold. "I mean, I …"

I laughed. "It's OK, Mari. I'm teasing, mostly. I'm a serial dater, aren't I? I didn't even realize it until now." I cringed. "Wow, I thought I had more self-awareness than that."

Her eyes were full of sympathy. "We all struggle to see some parts of ourselves realistically. I know that better than most people. But in your case … I mean, the term 'serial dater' isn't great. It sounds kind of bad. I think—" She stopped, her eyes uncertain now. "Do you want to know what I really think?"

"Always," I assured her. Well, the truth was, I was just like every other human being on the planet, and sometimes I wasn't in the mood to keep it real. A little denial never hurt anyone, right? *A little.* I almost laughed at my own rationalization, considering that one of my talents was to help others face their own thoughts and feelings—their truth. But Mariana had always needed lots of reassurance in this department, and I was happy to give it to her.

She took a deep breath. "OK. I think you're a hopeless romantic, so you want to be in love. But you're selective, and maybe you are afraid to commit. You always find reasons not to. But again because of the hopeless romantic thing, you keep trying. Over and over. Without really addressing the reasons it's not working out." Her eyes widened, and she clapped a hand over her mouth. "Oh my—Haz, I'm so sorry. That sounded terrible, and I didn't mean to—"

"Mari, it's OK. I can handle it." I offered a bright smile that I didn't feel on the inside.

Was she right? Was that really my problem? "How is it that *you*, who avoided all things emotions for *years*, until like a year ago, are so perceptive?" I forced a laugh.

She shrugged. "Am I wrong? I might be. As you said, I don't have a great track record." She paused and then continued more quietly, "If you disagree though, what part of it is wrong?"

And I couldn't think of a single thing.

Hopeless romantic? Check.

Selective? Maybe.

Afraid to commit? Um. Was I?

"I don't disagree—I'm just thinking about this. Like, how can a serial dater be selective? Especially in a small town like this?" I shook my head with a small smile.

"Correction. You're not that selective in the men you date. The selectiveness comes in a bit later, especially when things are going well and potentially progressing toward something more solid." She stopped, seeing my pained expression. "Like Brian from a month ago? You said he was perfect. I thought he was perfect. And then suddenly, you ended it."

I scoffed. "He snored! Really loud. I'm a light sleeper, so that's a dealbreaker."

"Or what about Jackson? The guy who moved here from Iowa? You told me he liked Pepsi, and you liked Coke. You broke him with him the day after Valentine's Day."

I nodded. "Well, that's true. We—"

"Beverage choices are not a reason to end a very promising relationship, Haz," she chided me gently.

I sighed loudly. "OK, I get it." My eyes searched hers for a long moment. "Mari, how long have you been thinking this? Why didn't you say anything?"

Her brows scrunched together. "It wasn't a fully formed opinion until recently. Terry and I were talking last week—"

"Wait, you guys talked about this?" I flinched.

She wet her lips before speaking slowly, "Just a little. He brought it up. He loves you like a sister, you know? We both do. We just want you to be happy."

My tone and no doubt my expression were doubtful. "Happy like you two? Mari, I think what you've found with him might be rare." I added more softly, "And I'm so glad you have him. You, more than anyone, deserve all the happiness in the universe."

She smiled wryly. "Not all. You deserve a massive portion of it too, Haz." Her expression changed as she looked away for the briefest of moments. "So, we didn't really get a chance to talk about this since I've been working insane hours in the post-Christmas rush, but did things go OK for you at the wedding reception? You seemed really out of sorts at the end. I asked Peter, since I saw you talking to him, but he just scowled and shook his head."

"He's not much of a talker, that one," I said dryly. "Yeah, we didn't exactly hit it off. In fact, it was hate at first sight. On his part. I wasn't his biggest fan either by the end of the night. He's a jerk, Mari. He wouldn't give me the time of day. I talked his ear off … like, to an embarrassing level. He barely responded and seemed annoyed, even angry. So rude. But whatever, I don't have time to waste thinking about jerks like him." OK, that part was a tiny lie, as I had thought about him a few times. Why, I don't know, as there was nothing pleasant about our interaction, and I was hoping I wouldn't see him again.

Her face lit up. "Well, that's what I thought of Terry a year ago, but look what happened!"

I grinned back at her. "You married your soulmate. And I still can't believe my best friend is now a *wife*. It's the best Christmas present I could've gotten, seeing your happiness as you walked down the aisle—before and after the ceremony. You were stunning. And the look in Terry's eyes when he saw you was … well, intense. That man is over the moon for you, Mari. And I love it. He's a good guy, our Mr. Pinecone, after all."

She giggled. "We're still calling him that?"

"Oh, absolutely."

"I guess that makes me Mrs. Pinecone?"

"Well, if you're taking his last name, but I thought you were more progressive than that." And we both burst out laughing.

"But seriously," I said, my tone more sober. "Peter is nothing like Terry. He's a cold, unfeeling—"

"OK, I get it. You don't like him. But he's Terry's best friend, you know? He's got to have some good qualities." Her brows furrowed. "I don't know him very well yet."

"I don't want to talk about Peter. He didn't even let me call him Pete. But Pete is such a great name!" I shook my head in wonder.

"All I'm saying is, Terry and I didn't exactly get along when we reconnected. I thought he hated me, and I kind of thought I hated him. But feelings can change—"

"Mari, seriously. You can't possibly compare them. You and Terry had *history*. You'd fallen in love ten years ago, and you never would've separated if not for his cold-hearted, scheming sister. Turned out you both had every reason not to get along when you met again—Blair screwed you both over."

Mariana shuddered. "Let's not talk about her. Even hearing her name makes me feel ill. She's just awful. We had to get a restraining order when she wouldn't leave us alone. I'm just glad she didn't try to crash our wedding."

"She's probably too broke now to afford a plane trip out here." She had, after all, been the sole reason the siblings had lost all their money, the entire inheritance they'd received after their parents' death over a decade ago.

Mari shook her head. "Oh, I'm confident she's not broke. Most likely she's shacked up with some unsuspecting fool, some rich guy she managed to charm."

"True." My lips curled up in the corners. "But the best part is, who cares?"

"Not me." She finished the last few sips of her tea and made a face. "My tea is cold. How long have we—oh, no. I told

Terry I'd get home by noon so we can finish packing." At my raised eyebrow, she laughed, but then her brows drew together in worry. "Is it OK if we head out to brunch soon?"

"Of course. The last thing I want is to delay your trip. I'll get ready fast—just give me just a few minutes." I rose and padded to the bathroom to brush my teeth and my hair, wash my face, and put on a knitted sweater and grey leggings.

When I stepped out of the bathroom, ready to go, I motioned for her to follow me to the front door. "Listen, Mari, I unloaded a lot on you today. But seriously, do not worry about me. Like you, I've been taking care of myself for a long time. I'll be fine. I'm honestly excited about making some changes. I've already got plans for three book ideas based on some of the more popular events I've spoken at." I paused, eyeing her uncertain expression as we headed outside. "Seriously, I am going to be great. And you two, go act like newlyweds. Enjoy your first vacation in, like, forever. And I'll see you in six weeks!"

Somehow, that little embellishment of my feelings and confidence gave me a boost of energy. There really was something to not only thinking positively but also saying it aloud. Of course, as I told all the lovely women who attended my tours, sometimes positive thinking is the worst thing you can do. Honoring your feelings and experiences is crucial.

But right now, I was optimistic. This would be a year of change, and I would embrace it like I did everything else.

"Hey world, get ready for the new Hazel!" I shouted, beaming at the bright sky above us once we reached the café.

Mari's eyes widened as she looked around us, seeing a few other people halt in their tracks to look at the crazy woman.

Me.

I giggled and gave her a long hug before heading home to go plan my new life.

Chapter 3

I was just waking from a blissful afternoon nap when I heard it.

The creaky double doors of a huge moving truck opening.

Boots crunching in the hard packed snow that fell last week.

Distant voices that sounded distinctly male.

Cursing under my breath, I removed my sleep mask and cap and squinted as I looked to the open window.

Dammit, I'd forgotten to close the window. When I'd gotten home from the gym this morning, I'd seen the most beautiful birds right outside my bedroom window. It was too cold to stand outside and watch them, but I opened my window to listen to their song.

Yeah, I wanted to listen to birdsong.

This was my life now. If I wanted to take the time to watch birds, I could. I was putting down roots for the first time. This was my home, but it was the birds' home first. Well, maybe not technically, since some birds have a short lifespan. Then again, I had a friend whose cockatiel was almost as old as I am.

It had been a month, and I was loving the change of pace, honestly.

But …

Sometimes loneliness crept in.

OK, it was not just sometimes. It happened a lot. I wasn't naturally a homebody, after all. Maybe I just needed to adjust, or maybe all this alone time wasn't fulfilling to me. I thought about renting a coworking space before laughing aloud to myself. As if Shipsvold had coworking spaces. The town was pretty old-fashioned, as one expects of quaint little places like this. But that was fine. I could learn to love my own company, surely.

Rubbing the sleep out of my eyes, I stood up slowly and then padded over to the window.

My eyes widened as I saw the scene before me, including not one but two enormous moving trucks. So, the new neighbor had a lot of stuff, eh? It was a pretty nice house, I have to admit. Nicer than the cozy two-bedroom I bought a few months back. But I was proud of my home and everything in it. It had all the markings of someone who was settling down. But in a good way, not in an "I settled for something less than I deserve" way. Because that was *not* what I was doing. I deserved—

My thoughts vanished as I saw a man emerge from the back of a truck and head into the house, large box in hand. He wasn't dressed in the collared shirts and grey vests worn by the moving company guys, so I assumed he must live there. I only saw his back, but he looked about my age, maybe a bit older. His hair was short and dark, and his clothes appeared well tailored and fit his solid physique like a glove.

Suddenly he started to turn around, and I ducked beneath the window. It wouldn't do for the new neighbor to see me as a creeper spying through the window. Even though I was.

I pressed my lips together, my thoughts racing. No one had lived in the house next door since I'd moved in. It was a large house with three stories and innumerable rooms. I'd heard the previous owner had set a high list price despite the place needing some work, so no one had been eager to buy it. Until now.

I should go bring him something. Or maybe *them*, as it could be a couple. Or a family. Or even some guys living together. The possibilities were endless. I snuck another look out the window quickly, hoping to see whether the man had a family with him, but I didn't see him or anyone else.

No matter. I'd make my famous sugar cookies. Or maybe my salted caramel brownies. Hmm. Or both?

No, both would be overkill.

I shook my head with a smile. Making both would be fun. I loved baking, and I was pretty decent at it too. Not enough to do it for a living, but people often asked me to bake for them.

That's what people did with new neighbors, right? Bring them a welcome basket or meal or treats or something? I thought so. Well, it was worth a try. No one could say no to my baked goods.

No one with taste buds, anyway.

I smiled while retrieving the recipes, which I *almost* knew by heart, but I didn't fully trust my memory because, well, that ended in disaster last time.

The cookies had been missing sugar, and I'd handed them off to Mariana without tasting one. How did I manage to not taste my own creations even once? Well, I was baking three other things that same day, and my body protested even the thought of more food. In any case, the attendees at Mari's staff meeting will never eat anything I make again.

Recipes in hand, I scoured the kitchen for all the ingredients. I thought about using this time to plan out the next chapter in my book. I'd written a couple chapters of background about my experience, and now I'd be diving into the good stuff, putting all my experience and know-how into the writing. The book was coming to life beautifully, and I couldn't be happier about it.

But no. Using this time to think about work ... well, no. Baking was meditative for me, and I needed a break from writing and *thinking* about writing. It's all I'd been doing, even when at the store, at the gym, at the gas pump. Everywhere.

With a satisfied smile, I started measuring out the flour.

I wished just once, though, that I could make anything with flour without making a giant mess. But nope. And I forgot to put an apron on, because of course I did. I made a mental note to change clothes before visiting the new neighbor.

Before I knew it, I was sitting on a kitchen stool tasting a cookie when I saw the pink, orange, and purple swirls out the window. How lovely, there's nothing more soothing than a sunset in a dusky sky. Maybe I could write about that.

Wait a minute. It's *that* late?

My brows furrowed as reality sank in. Apparently, I hadn't looked at the clock at all this afternoon. I'd hoped to visit the new neighbor earlier because, well, it's a little weird to bring over a welcome basket after dark, isn't it?

Now I didn't have a choice. These treats were amazing when fresh. They'd still be good tomorrow, but ... first impressions were important. If I finished up in an hour, I could take them over before it became *too* weird.

With that in mind, my blissful baking interlude was over, replaced by watching timers and deliberating over how many sweet treats to bring over. The man might live alone, or he might not. With such a large house, maybe he had six kids. I'd need to bring a lot of cookies to feed them all. A few dozen at least.

After placing another pan of cookies in the oven, I started selecting from the finished cookies and putting them in the parchment paper-lined wicker basket I'd found in the attic, making sure to leave space for the caramel brownies still cooling.

When the oven timer sounded, I turned it off and scanned the room for the oven mitt.

The soaring notes of Whitney Houston suddenly filled my ear, and I whirled around to find my phone. As the volume increased, I winced, wishing I'd turned it down earlier after my shower. Finally, I found it under a recipe and a box of foil on the counter.

"Papa, hi!"

"Aw, Hazy-chan, you answered!"

I grinned at my father's nickname for me. *Hazy* usually meant he was in a good mood, and *-chan* was his Japanese addition. Of course, good moods have been common since he moved back to Japan. I frowned at the thought. It was selfish, but I always wondered why he couldn't be happier *here*, with *me*. I shook my head to clear my thoughts. "Of course I answered. I always do, Papa."

"No, no. You didn't answer last time."

I paused, trying to remember. "Oh, I was at the dentist last Monday."

"So? You don't bring your phone there?"

I chuckled. "Well, yes, but I can't take calls. You have to put your phone on silent—Papa, you know this. You lived here for two decades; surely you remember what it's like to go to the dentist here."

"That was before cell phones," he muttered. Then, in a more pleasant tone, he asked, "How's my little girl? You finished writing that book you mentioned in text?"

I sputtered, "Uh, no—Papa, I just started a couple weeks ago. It takes time to write books. Especially nonfiction ones."

"Why?" His tone was innocent, but I sighed. Did he *ever* even try to understand my life and interests? "Never mind that. What are your holiday plans?"

I blinked a few times. "My plans—what holiday?" I chuckled. "Dad, the holiday season ended about a month ago."

"*That* holiday, yes," he grumbled. I'd apparently touched a nerve, as his odd obsession with Christmas was unmatched. "Valentine's Day, Hazy-chan."

I closed my eyes, wishing I were having any other conversation. "Oh, I for—" I stopped myself. "I have just been busy writing, you know?"

"Well?"

"Well what, Papa?"

"What are you doing to celebrate?"

"I—um, well ..." I trailed off. The truth—that I had forgotten the holiday was coming soon and had no plans of celebrating this year—would break his holiday-obsessed heart. "I haven't decided yet," I lied.

I bit my lip.

I couldn't lie.

"Actually, I might sit this one out," I said, hearing a slight tremble in my voice.

"*What?*" My dad was usually soft-spoken, at least with me. "Hazel, what do you mean?"

He hadn't misunderstood me. His English was fantastic, as he'd been a professional legal translator before retiring. I sighed. There was nothing to do but tell him the truth. All of it. "I'm taking a break this year, Papa. From the holiday and … well, from dating."

I heard his gasp. "I don't understand. Don't you want to—"

"No, I am just going to enjoy being single for a while."

He scoffed. "Enjoy being single? But you've always been single. Isn't it time for you to settle down?"

I breathed out shakily. It always came back to this. Sometimes I wondered if he wanted to see me get married just so he didn't have to think about me. So, in his mind, someone else would be responsible for me, taking care of me. "There's no hurry. I'm a grown woman. I can take care of myself," I choked out. "I *am* taking care of myself. I'm even—"

I caught a whiff of that distinct scent of something burning and whipped my head around. "Oh my god, I have to go," I exclaimed, fumbling around in the drawer for another oven mitt since I'd misplaced the other one. "Dad, sorry, I'm baking and burning something—got to go."

I hung up, nearly slipping on the floury surface of the floor as I raced toward the oven. Bracing myself, I opened it carefully.

Smoke poured out, causing me to step back. Hoping my oversensitive smoke alarm wouldn't go off, I opened the nearest window.

Closing my eyes, I gripped the counter as memories flooded through me. The disappointment obvious in Mom's eyes. The clenched hand that she quickly hid behind her. Biting her lip until I saw a trace of blood before she turned and fled the room. And then—

My heart in my throat, I shook my head wildly. *Focus, dammit.*

I *hated* burning things. I mean, no one liked burning a good batch of cookies. But for me, it was … well. I wasn't going to think about that.

Focus, Hazel.

I cracked a window and put the overhead fan on, grateful the alarm hadn't gone off yet. As the smoke dispersed, I walked back to the oven to remove the ruined cookies. Pausing for a moment, I wondered what to do with them until I remembered there was still some snow outside.

Outside they'd go, pan and all.

I sunk into a chair on my back porch, surveying the scene.

What a disaster.

It wasn't even the burnt cookies.

Or the memories …

Or even the difficult conversation about my love life, or lack thereof.

But I bristled at the reminder that my dad was so enamored with U.S. holidays and all things American—*yet* he'd moved back to Japan. Left me here … and everything he loved about this country. Was I the reason he left? It was ridiculous, but the thought came unbidden at the worst times. I squeezed my eyes shut and breathed deeper to prevent the tears from coming.

After my breathing returned to semi-normal, I gazed over at the house next door. Lights were on in several lower-level rooms, but the rooms upstairs were dark. I inhaled the cool evening air and gathered my strength to stand. Because I always keep going, no matter what. I don't have time in my life to wallow, nor do I have the interest. Certainly not when it comes to my parents and, well, what a disappointment I must be to them.

Opening the sliding door to reenter my house, I sighed. Onward was the only path. Even when it hurt. I saw the notification light on my phone but ignored it, choosing instead to bite into a soft, gooey brownie. I thought about pouring some wine before remembering I'd thrown it out. Oh well, it didn't sound that appealing anyway.

Who knows, maybe the new neighbor would be hot. From my view behind him earlier today, it definitely seemed possible.

Wait, you're not dating. It's better if he's not hot.

I shook my head. It didn't matter if he was hot. He was just a neighbor. And he probably had a wife and kids, maybe a dog … though I'd heard no barking all day. Maybe he liked exotic pets, like birds or snakes.

Maybe I should stop theorizing and find out. I laughed at myself while putting the treats in the basket and then grabbed my coat before sliding my feet into my thick winter boots.

I lugged the heavy basket using both arms as I carefully walked through the icy packed snow between my house and the neighboring house. Maybe I went overboard on the baked goods, but oh well. There were worse things, right?

It was fully dark out now, and I hoped the neighbor(s) wouldn't mind a late visitor. Stepping onto the large, wrap-around porch, I walked up to the door and looked for a doorbell.

None.

Hmm.

But an ornate brass knocker featured prominently on the massive front door, so I reached out hesitantly, taking a steadying breath before rapping softly and then a bit harder.

As I waited, I looked more closely at the knocker and saw an inscription with fancy lettering.

B.S.

Initials? I squinted and stepped closer.

Yes, it said B.S.

I started giggling as I ran my hand over the inscription on the metal.

Suddenly, the door opened before I could step back.

I gasped. "Oh!" I stepped back, recovering my breath as I stared at the man before me. My eyes fell to his body first, clad in black shorts and a loose blue T-shirt. His calves were nicely rounded, and my appreciative gaze found his hand, which had no wedding ring. "Uh, hi. Hello! I wanted to—"

My eyes met his and widened as my mouth fell open. "You —" Clamping my hand over my mouth, I stared at him and then squeezed my eyes shut. This can't be. It *can't* be—

"What are you doing on my porch?" came a familiar voice, sounding rough from lack of use.

"I ..." I stared at his icy blue eyes framed by thick lashes and a face that—well, it could be beautiful if it wasn't permanently grumpy. RGF. Resting grump face. My mind raced as I tried to remember details about the wedding reception when we'd talked. I'd had *way* too much to drink, but I remembered most of it. He'd taken an instant dislike to me, which was odd because most people liked me. I was so *not* an arrogant type, but I tended to make a good first impression with people. I'd been told I had some kind of natural charisma. Or maybe I'd just spent too much of my youth trying to please others, so it became a skill. I frowned at this thought, first suggested by a counselor during college.

The man cleared his throat.

I pasted on a smile. "Hello, Pete. Welcome to the neighborhood?" I hadn't intended that to sound like a question, but ... what the hell? What was *he* doing *here?*

A muscle tensed in his cheek. "Peter."

"Oh, uh ... OK. Peter. So, you're moving in here ..."

His eyes gave away nothing as he stared at me. "Clearly."

I bit my lip. "So that means we'll be—" I tried not to flinch. "We'll be neighbors? I live—" I stopped, pointing vaguely in the direction of my house. "There. I mean, I live next door. Ergo, neighbors."

Did I just say *ergo*? For the first time in my life.

His face remained completely devoid of any expression. "It appears so."

His hair was wet. I remembered it had looked light brown last time, but the water made it look dark. Oh wow, he must have just showered, given the wet hair and what looked like possibly pajamas. His feet were clad in dark slippers. I swallowed as my eyes took in his muscular legs again, and I wondered—

He cleared his throat again, interrupting my reverie. "Again, what are you doing on my porch?"

My eyes flew to his, and my face was on fire when I realized I'd been caught checking him out. Crap. No, I was just … sizing him up. Yeah, because he was an enemy?

No, I couldn't think that way. If we were neighbors now—neighbors!—we'd need to get along. I'd need to make some effort. Even if he didn't appreciate it at first. I forced my lips to curve upward. "I wanted to welcome my new neighbor. I brought a welcome gift …" I pointed at the oversized goodie basket sitting on the porch floor next to me. "I didn't know my neighbor would be *you*."

One eyebrow rose almost imperceptibly as the rest of his face remained stoic. "Is that a problem?"

My brows furrowed for a moment. "No, I didn't mean that. I just—I was surprised, that's all. What are the odds, you know? I thought you were doing some bigwig job in Chicago."

He put his hands in his shorts pockets. "I was."

"Oh." Well, he didn't want to share much—that was fine. I didn't care anyway. "Anyway, I'm a bit of a baker. So I brought cookies and brownies to welcome the new neighbors. I baked quite a lot, not knowing if a big family was moving in …" I tried to look past him but could see very little. "Is it just you, or—"

"Yes."

I swallowed, feeling frustration rising. He didn't like to talk, that much was clear. I managed to offer another smile, though it was almost physically painful. "So, welcome to Shipsvold, I guess. It's just me, you, and Doris across the street. No one else for a half-mile or so. And Doris is retired, so she's left for the winter. You won't meet her March, or maybe even April. So, you're stuck with just me. I hope you like baked goods! I mean, who doesn't, right?"

Dammit, I was rambling. Why did I always ramble in his presence? Apparently even when sober. If anything, I should keep things brief, like he did. But for some reason, his silence caused me to want to spew every thought.

He looked at the basket doubtfully, and then his eyes swept over me, stopping briefly on my midsection.

I glanced down and groaned. With flour everywhere, I looked like a powdered donut. Changing my clothes hadn't even occurred to me before I raced over here. I wondered if I also smelled like smoke from earlier. Shaking my head, I cursed my carelessness. So much for good impressions. "I mean, if you don't want them, I'll try not to be too offended. But just so you know, they're delicious. I've never had any complaints."

When his eyes met mine again, they were blank yet again, but he shook his head slightly.

I couldn't stop my frown this time. "Well, if you don't want them, I'll just take them back. I'm not going to force—"

He reached out to grab the basket and hastily set it down inside the house behind him. "Thank you," he muttered.

"You don't sound excited. But you haven't tasted them yet. Trust me, they're to die for."

"Well, I don't want to die."

Was he cracking a joke? A glance at his expression didn't reveal anything. I smiled though, hoping he'd been joking. "It's like paradise in your mouth." I sealed my mouth shut after that, immediately regretting the overly familiar, sensual language.

He just stared at me and slowly parted his full lips to speak. "Right. Is that all then?"

"I mean, yeah, that's why I came over," I said, my voice a bit salty. Had he never met a friendly neighbor before?

He scowled and put his hand on the doorknob. "I'd like to close the door now. It's cold."

My eyes widened. The man was just rude!

Then again, it was the middle of winter, and he was wearing shorts and a T-shirt while holding the door open while we talked. Of course he was cold. It was thoughtless of me to not notice.

But he could've invited me in too.

Why would he though? He didn't like me. At all.

"Ah, yes, I will go. I'm sure you have better things to do

than chat up the new neighbor, right?"

He nodded briefly and stood back to close the door.

"Um, OK, good night?" He was just going to shut the door without saying anything?

His hand on the door paused, but he didn't make eye contact. "Goodbye," he said firmly before the door closed and a lock clicked in place.

Chapter 4

Well. That went … not well.

I had half a mind to pound on the door and demand that he return my cookies and brownies. He didn't deserve my best creations. The man was unbelievably rude. Cold, even.

And I had to live next door to this guy? Though my teeth were chattering from the icy wind, my blood was boiling as I stomped back over to my house. Just before stepping into my house, I glared over in the direction of his house, as though he could see. But surely he wasn't spying out the window like I had been.

I kicked off my boots and threw my coat on the nearest chair before sinking into my soft lavender couch. Clutching a fuzzy throw pillow to my chest, I took some slow breaths to try to calm myself.

And then I promptly tossed the pillow across the room.

What—*who* did he think he was? How could a guy like *that* run a successful company or whatever it was he does? Or did, maybe. He was, after all, in a small town now, far from whatever Chicago business he was running. Maybe he was working remotely though. But why move *here*?

I rubbed my jaw, which was suddenly sore. I'd probably been clenching it for quite a while.

Though I was loathe to admit it, it made sense that he wasn't too impressed with me at the wedding. I was rambling, he was basically a stranger, and who knew how drunk I'd been at that point. But tonight? I was making a nice gesture. Not only was he totally ungrateful, but he acted as though I was poisoning the air around his new house.

I took a deep breath then. Ugh, he's not worth all this.

As my heart rate finally slowed, I started thinking back to his initial reaction upon answering the door. Had I surprised him? I frowned. He actually didn't seem surprised. Well, it's not as though his face was ever very expressive, but I wondered if he'd known I lived next door. But why then …

Oh no. No, no, no. He could've seen me spying through my window earlier. My face flamed as I wondered how much lower his opinion of me could have sunk.

But wait, *why* did he dislike me in the first place? Because I overshared at the wedding? Come on. People drink too much and do stupid things at weddings. Indignation coursed through me, followed by pain as I accidentally bit my cheek.

Cursing loudly, I went to the kitchen to find some ice to suck on. When I sunk back into the couch, I pulled a blanket over my body and around my shoulders. I would *not* let him get to me.

There was no reason to care what my neighbor thought.

Though he was not just my neighbor. He was also my best friend's husband's best friend. I sank deeper into the cushions with the thick knitted blanket as I realized the inevitable: we'd have a lot more social situations with him if he lived here now.

Not *if* he lived here. He obviously did.

But *why*?

I'd surely have to face him again, but not anytime soon. It was freezing outside, so I wouldn't see him out there. And Mari and Terry were still on their honeymoon, so I wouldn't get roped into any awkward social situations with them.

Until then, I'd hole up in here and be productive. I was used to not having a neighbor, other than Doris down the road, so I'll just … pretend I still don't.

*****

Avoiding interactions with my grumpy neighbor turned out to be easy. It was a colder February than usual, so I had no desire to step outside, apart from getting the mail. I was working out at home these days, as I hated the crowded gym in January and February of every year, when New Year's resolutions were fresh.

Avoiding *seeing* my grumpy neighbor was not so easy though. He was apparently a walker, as I saw him taking an outdoor walk every afternoon. When I'd first moved in here months ago, I'd arranged my writing desk in front of my living room window with a view of the road and the thickly wooded area in the distance. For weeks, I'd enjoyed the pleasant view, the sun appearing to warm the frigid landscape, rolling hills, and forest. But now, I saw *him*. Every day, he was out there walking, even when it was well below zero.

I had to admit to being surprised. I wouldn't have pegged him for the daily walking type. He seemed more like a runner or maybe even a triathlete, probably a competitive one because he seemed like that type. Not that I disliked runners—I'd had some great friends who were also marathoners, but the ones I'd dated happened to be jerks.

I sighed, looking at the mess on all the kitchen countertops. I'd had a bit of writer's block this week, leading me to bake. A lot. Fortunately, I had a deep freezer to store excess treats. And a well-stocked pantry, so I didn't often run out of things. I'd managed to avoid leaving the house for the past week. And … I should've felt good about that.

Avoiding the jerk next door was my goal, and I'd succeeded. Mostly, if I didn't count the grumbling to myself when he walked by each day.

Yet I didn't feel great. A sense of something—not quite loneliness, but similar. A sense of restlessness and dissatisfaction. I'd never stayed home and seen *no one* for this long before. All my life, I'd been on the go, whether moving around with my family growing up, being a busy working college student, or traveling for work. Just staying put felt uncomfortable. Maybe it was just new. Like all things, I'd get used to it.

I sighed as I finished wiping the counter and looked around for the broom, which I knew I'd left out after yesterday's similarly messy kitchen adventures.

But I was saved from further cleanup by a phone call. Well, more precisely, a video call. I smiled when Mariana's face flashed on the screen.

"*Haz*! You answered, and you're home! I'm so glad." Her hair was in a ponytail—which I'd never seen before—and she removed her sunglasses to reveal bright eyes.

I tilted my head and scrunched my eyebrows together. "Of course, why wouldn't I?"

"Well, you're just so busy, rarely at home, you know?"

"Oh … right." Yeah, that was my former life. "New Hazel is a bit of a homebody, I'm afraid. Even more in the last week because you would *never* believe—" My words faded as Mariana moved over to make room for Terry in the camera view. "Oh, hi Terry." I forced a smile. "I got to say, honeymoon looks good on you two."

I watched her cheeks redden, and she snuck a smile in Terry's direction.

"I have to agree. I mean, look at her … my wife. She's gorgeous," he said with a grin and a side glance toward Mari.

Feeling like a third wheel, I grinned back and gave an awkward thumbs up.

Mari's brows furrowed slightly. "Hazel, how are you doing?"

"I am great," I hurriedly reassured them both, my eyes going back and forth between them. "It's been so wonderful having some time to write and just … be."

"I'm happy to hear that," she said, with an expression that didn't quite look happy. "So you've written a lot then?"

I nodded. "Mm-hmm. Every day." Never mind that some days it was only, like, a sentence or two.

A smile played at Terry's lips. "Doing a lot of baking?"

"As a matter of fact—" I halted, seeing Mari's expression. Sheepishly, I asked, "So, even Terry knows I stress-bake?"

"And sad-bake and angry-bake and procrastinate-bake and—"

I rolled my eyes. "We get it, Mari. OK, yes, I have had a little writer's block occasionally.

More like every day.

Especially in the afternoons.

"Your freezer's full, isn't it?" Without waiting for an answer, Mari directed another pointed question at me. "When's the last time you left the house?"

"I have stayed home a lot, yes. But unlike the Mediterranean, here in frozen-town, Minnesota, it's cold as hell. Er, OK, that didn't make sense, but you know what I mean. Frigid. Frostbite within seconds—the weatherman said to stay home." Well, they'd said that last Sunday, when there was a wind chill warning.

Mariana and Terry were silent for a long moment, concern written all over their newly tanned faces. Well, slightly tanned but mostly freckled in Mari's case.

I shook my head and sighed. "Just say it."

"You have cabin fever, Haz," Mari pronounced, while Terry nodded next to her.

"No, I don't. I—yes, I've been home a lot, but it's nice. Being home. Staying in one place." This is what I wanted.

"I know you were looking forward to staying in one place for a while. I get that. But not literally staying at home 24/7. That's not you. You're not a hardcore introvert like I am, Haz."

"Definitely not," Terry said, giving me a sympathetic smile.

Were they right? I thought my problem had just been plain old writer's block, amidst the larger career shift I'd made recently ... and my best friend being out of the country.

I nodded slowly. "I guess you're right. Well, it *is* freezing here."

"Well, how about—" She stopped, looking sideways. "Terry, what's that weekly winter social thing they have down at the village?"

"Honey, we literally own the place. You should know this."

She waved her hand dismissively. Social events had never been important to Mari. But I knew what she was talking about, as I'd gone there with friends or the odd date here and there.

"I forgot about that," I said honestly. "I guess I haven't felt that social, you know? And it's *cold.*"

"There's a huge bonfire," Terry pointed out with a grin. As though he was being helpful.

I shook my head. "No, I don't know. I—" I stopped and took a long breath. "Fine, maybe I'll go next time. Not making any promises though." I crossed my arms in front of my chest.

"Hazel, you're not yourself. Even Terry can see it." Mariana's eyes bored into mine for a long moment, or three. She looked over at Terry with an expression I couldn't read.

He gave her a tiny nod and turned back to me. "So, I got news."

My lips curved upward, hoping this subject was finally closed. "Oh, do tell."

"My best bud from Chicago—my best man in the wedding, remember? He's moving to Shipsvold!"

He looked so genuinely happy that I tried with all my might to keep the smile pasted on my face. "Ah. That is … that's great for you guys."

A look passed between them before Mari added, "I think he's already moved there actually. Didn't he say the 1st of February?"

Terry nodded. "Oh, right. He did say that. Then he's already in town!"

"A normal friend would've given you that update," Mari said to her husband in a teasing tone.

"Hey, he's a great guy, a great friend. But not so communicative, that's true," Terry said with a laugh. "Anyway, yeah, it's pretty exciting."

I thought carefully about my response. Should I act clueless? Admit I'd already seen him? Mention he was *living next door*?

Another thought passed through my mind: Were *they* pretending to be clueless? Trying to see if I'd admit to having encountered him already?

I bit my lip, unsure which path to take.

"I'm happy for you, Terry." There, that's fair. I didn't lie—I just omitted the tiny fact of our meeting last week. Or was it the week before last? The days had started to run together.

"I heard he didn't make the best impression with you, but give it time." At my doubtful expression, he chuckled. "He's actually a great guy. And he's been through a lot."

I must have raised my eyebrows because Mariana jumped in. "Seriously, Hazel. You just got off on the wrong foot. I think your next meeting will be better. In fact, maybe the two of you could hang out at the weekend bonfire thing. Just break the ice a bit."

Terry smiled at her double entendre, while I balked. "Uh, what? He doesn't exactly seem like the casual bonfire hangout kind of guy. Isn't he like ... a strait-laced Wall Street type or something?"

Terry frowned, while Mariana shrugged. "I mean, he could be both? Sure, he does seem a tad uptight when you meet him. It's true, Terry," she said, looking at him quickly. "But maybe he moved here to try to make some changes."

I couldn't help it; I laughed. "I'm sorry, it's just—he's still —" I clamped my mouth shut then before I could say any more. "Look, I appreciate you guys trying to get me out of the house and stuff, but I'm fine. And once you're back, I'll be even better. When are you coming back again?" I asked with a hopeful note in my voice.

"Next week," he said with a mournful look.

Mariana nodded, her face also looking distinctly regretful. "Don't get me wrong—we miss you and the town and the resort and everything. But these past five weeks have easily been the best of my life." She grinned. "And you know I'm not the sentimental type."

I smiled wistfully. "So much truth in that statement. And yet there you are. I'm so happy for you, Mari. You deserve all this happiness and more. You know that, right?"

She nodded slowly. "I do now. And you deserve it too, Haz. Don't give me that look. You do! I know you're not dating right now, but—"

"I'm *so* sick of talking about me. I want to hear about Italy! It's one of the few places in the Northern Hemisphere I've never been, so I need all the details. Well, maybe not *all* the details—let's keep it PG, all right?"

Mari's face colored again, and I laughed. Even when she was the queen of avoiding and concealing emotions, her blushing often gave her away. Oh, I really missed my best friend.

"Ah, we actually have to go soon, Haz. I'm sorry," she said, her mouth scrunching to one side. "One thing I miss about our country is the prevalence of free Wi-Fi. Not a thing in Europe, we've learned. This call is costing us a fortune."

I flinched. "Oh no, Mari, why didn't you tell me?" I mean, I should've known. I'd spent plenty of time in Europe myself, especially during holidays with my jet-setting mother.

"*No*, it's been totally worth it! But we should probably not run up the bill any more," she said with a nervous laugh, and Terry nodded. "We are going to have an epic catch-up session when we're back though. Or several. You're going to get sick of me, Haz."

"Not likely," I said fondly. "But you go enjoy your day."

At least one of us should. I sighed but offered another convincing smile before ending the call. At least I hoped it was convincing. I'd need to work on my facial expressions—apparently I was easy to read these days. And that shouldn't bother me, but ... well. I wasn't always the open book everyone expected me to be.

Chapter 5

Staring at my reflection in the mirror covering the entire wall above the double sink, I leaned forward and squinted. Was that a silver hair near my right ear?

It was! I scrambled to find my tweezers in a drawer and then plucked out the offending strand. Wincing at the brief pain around my temple, I held it in front of me. It was only about an inch long, but it was definitely silver. Or grey. *Not* the sleek black it was supposed to be.

I sighed deeply. This was it. The beginning of the slow slide into aging and old maid status. I really thought I'd have a few more years before starting to grey, given my Japanese blood from my father's family. But my mother had started coloring her grey in her early thirties, so I supposed I was doomed.

Not that grey hair was somehow bad. In truth, I thought it was beautiful, and I'd admired many a woman with artful greying tones. My grandmother had had white hair for as long as I remembered, and she'd been one of my favorite people growing up. One of the only people who seemed to notice me.

My long, silky, black hair had often been called my best feature. And one grey hair didn't diminish that.

And I'd spent years preaching a doctrine of self-acceptance, beauty, body positivity, and vigor at all ages, and all of that. It was my livelihood.

Still.

Ugh.

I could pull off a silvery style. I was generally pretty

confident in my appearance, despite society's frequent messages that I shouldn't be as a short, curvy, multiracial woman.

Then why was this bothering me? I tried to put my finger on it as I brushed my long, dark locks slowly. Maybe because it felt like ... a clock was ticking. Like, maybe this was a new phase of life that I wasn't ready for. Maybe I had a lot more I wanted from life, and I wasn't there yet. But that should be fine because plenty of people accomplish a ton of stuff well past their thirties.

But some things had an expiration date. Having children, for one. I wasn't in a hurry to become a mother, but I always thought I would, eventually. After I fell in love and lived happily ever after. Everyone called me a hopeless romantic, and they were right. But for a romantic, I evidently had no idea how to find love for myself. I sighed loudly.

"Enough," I said aloud.

My gaze slid over to the clock on another wall, and my eyes widened. I still had to pack! I quickly put the finishing touches on my makeup and then changed into one of my many "business travel" outfits. I wasn't going on a plane, only driving my own car, but I could still look put together.

In an hour, I was leaving to drive to St. Paul for a meeting with my agent. So far, we'd only met virtually, but she wanted to introduce me to some important people and had even set up a meeting with the editor of a midsized publisher.

My lovely assistant, Roxy, had found a literary agent for me from the Franchersantz agency in the Twin Cities. Sofia Jackson had been looking to expand her nonfiction list, and when we met in a video call, we connected instantly. The vibe was natural, fun at times and serious at others, and Sofia was genuine, at times brutally honest, and always empathetic. My only experience with an agent was a few years ago when I published my one and only book with the help of my former agent, Sandy. She had been ... fine. Not great, but she got the job done. She sold my idea to a decent-sized publisher, and we had decent sales. But Sofia was on another level. As a fellow woman of color, she was one of the most confident people I'd ever met, at least outwardly with her killer smile, and I loved that she'd been championing other POC in her work even years before it became the popular thing to do. But more than anything, I loved that she was direct with me. Always kind, but always honest. That's what I needed more than anything, and I'd never really had that in my life.

I couldn't wait to meet her in person.

After hastily packing a small suitcase, I scanned my fridge for a snack for the road. I sighed when I saw how empty it was. It was long past time I ventured out to the grocery store. I needed to stop putting my life on hold for some stupid jerk that happened to live next to me. We could be neighbors, and maybe I'd be cordial since we had mutual friends. I could manage that, surely. I'd do anything for my best friend, even be nice to the grump ... or nice-*ish*.

I bit into the very last banana as I hauled my small suitcase and purse to the side door. My garage wasn't attached, but it was just a few yards from my house. I thought wistfully of my idea to someday pay a contractor to build a four-seasons room to connect the house to the garage. I could pay for it with my huge royalty check from all the books I'd be writing.

I laughed wryly. I already knew being a writer likely wouldn't pay many bills, but I had other business ideas to supplement my income, in addition to having saved a comfortable amount in the past few years. And writing books wouldn't pay *anything* if I didn't actually write them first.

I frowned while opening the wooden door and then the screen door, only to have it forcefully swing open and out of my grasp. In a split second, my face was covered in freezing, wet snow, and I instinctively reared back and closed the inside door.

What on earth! Since when was it snowing? I'd seen no signs of snow—not even a flurry—this morning while working at my window-adjacent desk. The sun had even made an appearance.

My mind raced as I went to grab a towel and dry off my face and hair. I moved the shades aside as I looked out my front window, my heart sinking at what I saw.

Nothing.

I couldn't see a damn thing.

Taking a deep breath, I reminded myself to stay calm. Freaking out wouldn't fix this. I walked over to the foyer to switch on the outside lights, thinking I'd already turned them on earlier.

Oh. I *had* turned them on earlier. They just weren't working.

I headed through the kitchen to the back door to look behind the curtain.

Thankfully, the back porch light had a switch just inside the door. After flipping the switch, I gasped. Even my large, covered porch was blanketed in snow drifts at least a foot high, with snow swirling around so fast and so high that I could barely even see the ceiling. The light fixture up there showed only a faint light through all the blowing snow. Beyond the porch, the view was cloudy white from what little I could see.

Letting the curtain fall back down, I leaned back against the pantry door.

Fu ... dge. Fudge, fudge, fudge.

Because one of my other resolutions was to stop swearing.

But if there was ever a time for profanity, it was now.

I wouldn't give in—*don't give in, don't give in. Don't break down. Don't freak out.*

Mmm, fudge—I could make some. Or maybe I could try making that chocolate and cream cheese lasagna I'd read about yesterday.

I was already tying my apron strings when I caught myself. *Wow, Hazel, stress baking is one thing, but this is a crisis.*

My mind went blank as my fingers itched to start gathering ingredients.

Think, Hazel. Think.

I forced myself to remove the apron and go sit at the dining table. I dug my phone out of my pocket as reality began to sink in. That was an all-out *blizzard* out there. How had I not known? I frowned, pressing the power button repeatedly on my phone before remembering I'd forgotten to charge it last night when I went to bed. It was dead.

I hurried to the bedroom to get my charger but paused to head over to the TV remote first. There was probably some local news and weather coverage I could get through my antenna. Then again, the antenna probably wouldn't be working in this weather. I continued on my way to the bedroom and then froze abruptly.

I was plunged into darkness, accompanied by a quick whirring sound and errant beeps from devices gasping their last breath.

Remaining rooted to the spot, I placed my arm on the hallway wall to steady myself. The thick silence and heavy blackness threatened to suffocate me until I heard a faint ticking sound.

It was the antique clock in the living room. I placed my hand over my thumping heart and attempted to breathe slowly. I'd survived many power outages before. And I'd lived in Minnesota for years, so snowstorms weren't new to me. But the nothingness felt overwhelming, especially with a blizzard surrounding my home, and it was a struggle to avoid all-out panic as I started slowly walking back to the living room. I could hear my pounding heart and big puffs of air as I tried not to not take shallow breaths. When I nearly tripped over something on the floor—perhaps a slipper—I gripped a wall nearby to steady myself.

Finally, I reached a drawer on an end table where I kept a flashlight. I heaved a loud sigh of relief as it switched on, illuminating the room. I'd never been so thankful for light, and my fingers wrapped around it in a tight embrace.

Placing my other shaky hand on the edge of the sofa, I sat down. I needed to think.

I needed to find some more flashlights and candles, and I had to get access to a weather forecast. The ticking clock began to torment me as I scrambled to get my thoughts together.

"I'll talk out loud. Yes, then it won't be so weird." I almost laughed. "OK, it's definitely weird, just in a different way."

My tablet! That didn't lose charge as quickly as my phone, so it probably still had some battery. I started to rise from the couch before plopping back down. Nope. Even if the tablet had a battery, it wouldn't have internet. No power meant no Wi-Fi.

I let out a loud groan and then instantly regretted it, realizing my voice sounded really creepy right now.

Well, maybe I could just take a nap. Surely the power will be back on soon, and then I could figure out what to do. I sensed this storm wasn't going to abate in time for me to drive to the Twin Cities—and who knew, maybe the snow was even worse there—so I'd need to contact Sofia as soon as I had power. Pulling a throw blanket over my body, I stretched out on the sofa, resting my head on a pillow. I loved naps, after all. Might as well take advantage of this downtime, right?

Wrong. Sleep was evasive with only the ticking clock serenading me. I usually slept with a fan, never in silence. I thought about smashing the clock to bits, but maybe absolute silence would be worse than that incessant ticking of time. Still, I sank further into the couch and under the blanket, hoping I could force some rest at the very least.

After some indeterminate amount of time—because I didn't wear a watch and couldn't see the clock from this position —I grimaced and sat up. Trying to sleep was pointless. And I was starving. I figured I shouldn't open the fridge with the power out, as the cold air needed to stay trapped in there as long as possible to avoid all my food spoiling. I grabbed a banana from the fruit bowl on the counter and leaned against the kitchen island. "At least I have running water," I whispered after finishing the banana and filling a glass.

But maybe not for long, I realized. If it's cold enough, without heat, the pipes could freeze.

I was at serious risk of bursting into tears, but so far my eyes were dry as I stared unseeing into the dimly lit room. I'd found a candle but no matches or lighter. Breathing in and out rhythmically, I tried to calm my mind so I could figure out what the heck to do.

It wasn't long before I realized the shaking wasn't just emotional; I was cold. The house couldn't be cooling this fast, could it? I cringed as I remembered writing "replace insulation" on my to-do list months ago.

"From now on, I'm going to do all house repairs ASAP. I swear! Just please, insulation, do me a solid and do your job tonight!"

Now I was talking to an inanimate object, one I couldn't even see. I sighed, shivering again, and then walked over to the back door to put on a yellow fleece jacket hanging from a hook. Looking out the window again, I decided to bundle up and brave the storm to see if the view was better from another side of the porch. With my boots, hat, and scarf covering as much of my body as possible, I unlocked the door and gripped it hard as I slowly pushed it open.

I needn't have worried about the wind whipping the door off the hinges, as there was a sizable snow drift barricading the door, and I had to use all my might to push it open even halfway. Attempting to ignore the frigid ice crystals pelting against my face, I strained to look with the flashlight beyond the porch roof to the left toward my garage, seeing nothing but thick, swirling snow as far as my eye could see, which wasn't very far. The wind was howling, and none of the woods behind my backyard was visible. It wasn't pitch black but more of a very opaque silvery grey.

I turned and pointed the nearly useless flashlight to the right, seeing more of the same—

Except ... what was that? I blinked a few times, trying but failing to wipe my wet lashes with my equally wet gloves.

A tiny faint light shone in the distance. It appeared to be flashing on and off, unless my eyes were deceiving me—which was quite possible.

Wait, that's ... *Peter's house.*

Or at least near his house.

My jaw hung open until I tasted snow on my tongue. I kicked some freshly blown snow out of my path back into the house and tugged the door closed again. Panting, I ripped off my wet winter gear and dashed over the couch, wishing I had a fireplace.

Peter probably has a fireplace. Or several, in that massive house that was *far* too big for just him.

But since it was big, maybe …

No.

No.

But …

No.

I bit my lip and face-planted into the nearest pillow.

The last thing I needed was to deal with that jerk. Even if it was cold and dark and a bit panic-inducing.

I pictured him for a moment with a room full of candles as he sipped a hot drink in front of a roaring fire, satisfied that *his* insulation was in good shape. He was probably even using his phone or other device at this moment, having had the foresight to charge them before the power went out. Because he'd probably seen the weather forecast and prepared—he seemed like that kind of guy. I scowled and then squeezed my eyes shut, trying to ward off the migraine headache that I knew was building.

My eyes flew open. Maybe he *was* that kind of guy, but that wasn't the worst thing right now. In fact, it was exactly what I needed. I could go take advantage of his warm house, at least to use his phone to find out what the hell was going on with the weather. Maybe—

No, Hazel. Forget this idea immediately.

I couldn't, because it was *him*. He'd probably turn me away and laugh about it. Well, if he was the kind of guy who laughed, and he clearly wasn't. But certainly he'd get some silent joy from telling me to get lost.

I shook my head, vowing not to even *think* about this idea anymore.

Chapter 6

I should've brought a shovel.

It would have been easier to take my time and shovel myself a path than to try to trudge through several feet.

Better yet, I should've brought a sled. Sleigh? Right, because it wasn't totally weird to think about owning a *sleigh* as a single adult in Minnesota. Was I becoming delirious? Clearly, I wasn't the best person to answer that.

I was deeply regretting my workout this morning. To procrastinate from writing, I'd taken advantage of my basement home gym more than usual lately. This morning's workout was mostly legs with a bit of cardio. And now ... well, now, my legs were screaming at me.

Finally, after what seemed like an eternity even though our houses weren't very far apart, I reached his large porch and trudged up the few steps. I gripped the icy railing to ensure I wouldn't slip because the last thing I needed was for him to find me half-buried in a heap of snow near his porch.

My heart was racing as I neared the front door. Regret coursed through me as I realized this was a stupid decision, but then I thought of how difficult it had been to walk here, and I steeled my spine.

Before I could rap on the door though, the thick wooden door started opening slowly.

I stepped back, my eyes wide as I saw him appear in the doorway, behind the screen.

His eyes went wide too, a rare bit of emotional expression,

as his eyes landed on mine and then scanned over me for just a moment before his face returned to its usual monotone emptiness. "Hazel?"

"Uh, hi, yes, it's me, Hazel," I managed to say. "Your neighbor." Captain Obvious here. He merely blinked, his face showing no expression. "So, hi … this storm is pretty bad, right?"

He nodded slightly and furrowed his brows. "It's dangerous. What are you doing out there?"

His deep voice held a note of anger, and I stared back at him. Was he angry at me? Seriously? Or maybe it was frustration at the whole situation, I thought generously.

"I, ah …" I stopped to remove my hat because the snow on it was dripping onto my face. But when his eyes widened again, I realized my mistake. My hair surely looked terrible under my soaked hat. Oh well, too late now. I tried to feign my usual confidence. "It's really bad, yes. And that's why … well, I was thinking … maybe …" And I just couldn't make myself say it.

After a beat of silence, he crossed his arms over his broad chest. "What?"

I wished I could blame my teeth chattering, but I really couldn't. I was afraid he'd turn me away. And *then* I'd be even worse off, having to return to my house *and* having put a massive dent in my pride.

Tell him why you came, Haz. You've dealt with far worse than this in your life.

I inhaled deeply, about to speak, but he beat me to it. "Do you need something from me?"

"I, uh, yes. I mean, maybe. If you want to," I said, flashing a smile to cover my ineptitude in basic speech. "Do you have any of those cookies left, or did you eat them all?"

His eyebrows rose no more than a millimeter. "You came here to ask me about the cookies?" He shook his head. "They're safe in the freezer."

"Ah. Like the rest of us, am I right?" Laughing a bit too loud, I nervously smoothed my hair.

"I don't understand," he said flatly, his eyes never leaving mine.

"I mean, we're all freezing because of … well, you know." I waved my hand behind me on my right. "This terrible blizzard. Never mind, bad joke."

His eyes bore into mine for a long moment as I tried to think of how to salvage this. Finally, he leaned his shoulder against the door and sighed. "If you came to partake of my hospitality, just say so."

It was then I noticed the lights on behind him. Not just the dim lighting of flashlights and candles but an apparently well-lit room off the front hall. "You have electricity?"

He nodded.

"But how—I assumed—oh, is it from a generator?" Why hadn't I thought of that? Well, of course I hadn't. I was great at many things, but being prepared for blizzards and power outages was not one of those things.

He nodded again, this time more slowly as if affirming the obvious. Then he stood up straight and waved an arm in front of him, motioning for me to come in as he opened the screen door. "Fine, just … come in, I guess." I was about to follow him and express my gratitude for all eternity when he let out a loud exhale, and I stopped in my tracks.

He turned. "Are you coming in or not? Make up your mind," he snapped. "Haven't you noticed, you're letting a lot of cold air and flurries in the house?"

Oh … I actually hadn't noticed. But what the hell? He was back to being a complete jerk now? Well, at least he'd spoken three sentences to me. That might be a record. I tried to swallow my pride and indignation and adopted a cheerful tone as I stepped into the house. "Well, I've got bad news for you, Pete. Given that I just walked through a blizzard, I'm basically one giant flurry myself. Where should I put my boots?" I looked around, not seeing a rug for removing footwear.

He stopped in his tracks and paused before turning around, his eyes boring into me as his jaw clenched. "My name is Peter. I don't answer to Pete or any other such *nickname*."

I swallowed with some difficulty. "Oh, right—you did tell me that, and I completely forgot. You know, it was …" I trailed off as he turned around and began to stride down the hall.

Screw this. What was this guy's deal? "Hey. Peter." When he slowed but didn't turn around, I added, "Wait."

Finally, he drew to a halt again and pivoted, and his loud sigh seemed to echo off the long, quiet hall. His lips were pressed in a thin line when his eyes met mine again. "What is it now?"

"You know, I think I'll just go back home. I don't want to intrude, and you're … well, you're busy or something. I'm clearly a burden. So, I'm just going back to my house now." I nodded quickly and then turned, my head held high as I fought to remain civil.

But he was by my side in a flash. "Don't be ridiculous. Your house has no heat or electricity. I assume that's why you're here. Only an idiot would go back when—"

My eyebrows shot up my forehead. "Only an idiot? Are you serious right now?" I shook my head. "You know, I would think since our best friends are married *and* we're neighbors now for some reason, you'd want to *try* to act less like a jerk. But apparently not. Maybe you're incapable." I inhaled and exhaled sharply. "But I'm out. This is the last thing I need."

"The last thing? I would think that it's the first thing," he said calmly, his face betraying no emotion. "You need a haven from the storm. That is why you came here."

I stared at him for a moment. "It is. But I made a mistake. I won't bother you again." Before he could respond, I opened the door and practically ran out onto the porch. But I had to grip the railing tightly to avoid slipping on the stairs, which had fresh snow on top of several layers of packed snow and ice, resulting in not only a slippery surface but also a slanted one.

I retraced my steps back as best I could, but it was still extraordinarily difficult to plod through the thick snow, which seemed even deeper now although I hadn't stayed at his house very long. I nearly fell face first but managed to stay upright, just barely.

After what seemed like an eternity, my legs screaming at me the entire time, I reached my house and practically dragged myself up the three small steps to the porch. I sighed with relief when I reached the landing, only to lose my footing and land flat on my bottom. I winced at the pain, which wasn't even that bad because of the soft padding of the fresh snow that had blown onto the porch. I bit my cold, wet lip and tried to stem the flow of tears building as I stood slowly and took careful steps to the front door.

Once inside, I slammed the door shut and took in the darkness and eerie silence. All that misery outside, only to be back here in a different kind of misery.

I peeled off my wet outer clothes and boots and tossed them on a chair. Realizing *all* my clothes were wet, I pulled them all off, desperate to get the cold, wet, clammy items away from my body.

Now, of course, I was shivering so hard I could barely walk, but I set out to find the bathroom by clinging to the wall to orient myself in the dark, since I had no idea where the flashlight went. Finally reaching the bathroom, I felt around the back of the door and sighed loudly when reaching it. My thick pink robe!

My teeth chattering, I pulled it on, wiped my face and hands with a hand towel, and then grabbed some extra towels from the bathroom cabinet before slowly finding my way back to the living room.

It was only then I realized my face was damp with fresh tears.

No, Hazel. No time for tears. Think!

I wiped my eyes in frustration.

Didn't I have some more flashlights somewhere? Or other battery-operated light sources? Surely, there were—

Well, I had a few motion-activated lamps that ran on batteries in the basement. But the thought of going down into the cold, dusty basement in complete darkness was so unappealing I immediately dismissed the idea. I stared blankly into nothing as my spirits fell somehow even further.

Think, Hazel. You're a resourceful, independent woman.

But I couldn't think. Panic gripped me, and I sat motionless except for the incessant shaking because I was cold, so cold that I felt I'd never be warm ever again.

Somewhere through the brain fog came a startling realization. A lightsaber! *If* it came with batteries, that is. I shot up from the couch and walked toward the kitchen where I knew the island was. I almost made it before smashing my toe into a stool. Flinching at the instant pain, I was grateful to still be somewhat numb, as it should've hurt more than it did. And then, my hand connected with the toy, and I almost cried in relief.

Jeff, the financial advisor from the resort, had a daughter who was turning eight next weekend, and she was obsessed with all things Star Wars, so I'd ordered this gift for her and intended on wrapping it today.

But my heart sank when I realized this would be incredibly difficult, if not impossible, to open in the dark. Plastic packages like this usually required scissors, and I didn't trust myself to use one in the pitch blackness. I sank into the stool and cradled my head in my arms on the counter.

I didn't know whether to cry or scream, so I did both. I couldn't catch a break tonight. This was one of the worst—

Suddenly a pounding on the door awakened my senses further. My heart rate skyrocketed, and I opened my eyes wide even though it did no good.

Someone was here.

Oh my god, someone was *here*.

What if it was a burglar? I had no protection, not even the use of my vision to help me. And I doubt I could see anything out of my window. I walked slowly toward the front door, holding the toy package in my hand in case I needed a weapon—it was better than nothing.

But wait. What if it was someone helpful, like a friend checking on me? Or the police? They could be here to save me!

I'd better check—wait, no. How the hell would they have gotten here? No way are those roads passable right now. It must be someone nefarious, someone—

"*Open the door!*" shouted a muffled voice, followed by another loud knock that seemed to shake the house.

I gulped down a few breaths, shaking harder than before. I could handle this. I'd just knock them out if they managed to get into the house.

"*Hazel, open up, dammit!*"

Wait, the invader knew my name? How on earth … oh.

Oh.

My rude, arrogant, jerk-face neighbor.

I let out a breath very slowly, lowering my makeshift weapon. I considered not answering the door, but he sounded determined and … well, maybe he came over to apologize and offer a flashlight or something. One could hope, right?

I walked to the door slowly, flinching as my bare feet landed on the drenched rug. After unlocking and swinging the door open, I blinked at the bright light but said nothing as my eyes met Peter's.

Holding a lantern, he was dressed head to toe in black winter gear, stark against the dusky white of the drifting snow on the porch. He took a step forward, and I didn't think fast enough, because instead of telling him to back off, I jumped backward. He took advantage of the space to step into my house.

As he took off his thick black knit cap, his harsh voice intruded on the quiet. "What on earth took you so long to—" His words died on his lips as his eyes began to skim over me.

He swallowed and then shook his head. "You're freezing. Put some clothes on," he said harshly. "You answer the door like this? I could've been a thief or murderer or worse."

I laughed despite my predicament. "Who else would be out in this nightmare weather? You were shouting through the door, so I knew it was you. And it's pretty obvious you're not going to murder me or ravish me or steal—" I stopped at his raised eyebrows. "Or, um, *are* you here to kill me?" I backed away a bit, gripping the lightsaber.

The corner of his lips twitched so faintly I might have

imagined it. "Well, if I am, I don't think a toy weapon is going to save you."

I glared at him. Was he actually making a joke? Unmoved, I crossed my arms over my chest. His eyes flickered down and then returned to glaring back at me.

After a painfully long moment, he sighed loudly. "You forgot your hat," he said while handing it to me.

Snatching it out of his hand, I retorted, "Obviously." Likely my hair was not only wet and matted down but also a mess of long tangles. Not my best look, but then, why should I care? This man was nothing to me.

His eyes scanned the room. "Have you just been sitting alone in the dark? Don't you have any flashlights at least? Candles? Clothing?"

These were fair questions. I didn't have answers, other than the fact that I'd been struck by panic rendering me nearly immobile. My lips trembled a bit as I whispered, "I lost the flashlight and ..." I paused to take a steadying breath. "I was about to look for more when you—"

"Hazel," he said, gritting his perfect white teeth. "Stop being stubborn. Just come back to my house and stay there." His eyes bore into mine before he added, "Until the storm abates or the power outage resolves. Surely the electric company will fix things soon, right?"

I scoffed. "You're not from a small town, are you? It could take hours. Or days. Depending on the storm."

Oh my god, it could take *days*.

I couldn't do this for *days*. It had only been ... maybe two hours? I had no idea.

I had no choice though. There was no way I'd go with *him*.

Straightening my shoulders, I stood as tall as I could, which wasn't very tall. "I'll stay right here, thank you very much."

His face remained impassive, but I thought his eyelid twitched, or it might have been a trick of the shadows.

"I'll be fine. I'll figure out how the fireplace works. Don't need electricity for that, right?" I hadn't ever used the fireplace because my body tended to run warm. But a contractor had informed me when I moved in that the fireplace was in working order.

"You don't know how to use the fireplace?" He looked genuinely confused. "And you're going to figure it out in the dark? Do you have wood to burn?"

"Uh, *yeah*." No, I didn't, but there was no way he'd find out. "Of course."

His eyes narrowed. After a long moment, his face returned to the expressionless mask I was used to now. "You're completely unreasonable. But I won't force you." He looked down at the lantern in his hand and then back at me before holding it out to me. "I'll go. Here, take the light."

My eyes widened as I searched his face, which looked resigned. "You want me to—oh, no, I couldn't."

"I have a generator, Hazel. I don't need this."

"But the walk back to the house—"

"I'll be fine. You, however, will not."

I gasped. "You're so rude. Has anyone ever told you that?"

He merely blinked. "Yes."

I opened my mouth to speak but wasn't sure what to say. "Oh. Well. You are."

He nodded as though this wasn't news. "Take the lantern."

With my lips tight, I shook my head. "No."

"Stubborn—"

"Just go, Peter."

He stared at me for a long time, his cool blue eyes revealing nothing while his tight jaw suggested he was frustrated. Maybe even irritated. Finally, he carefully set the lantern down and walked out the door.

Chapter 7

My mouth gaping, I watched him through the open screen door swung wide open by the whipping wind. It took a moment to find words. "Hey, take this lantern —" But the words died on the wind, and he was already off on the makeshift path between our houses.

Gripping the door, I pulled it shut as hard as I could, slammed the wood door closed, and then set the offending light source on the floor just inside. My feet were wet again from the drenched rug, so I stepped a few feet away onto the carpet runner leading to the living room.

With a deep sigh, I crossed my arms over my chest as a shiver worked its way through my entire body. It was cold in here, I realized as the heat of indignation slowly faded. The temperature was dropping, and having that entire exchange with the front door open was probably the culprit.

I was *not* going to use the jerk's lantern.

Kneeling down, I looked for the off switch on his fancy LED light. But just before turning it off, I paused with my finger hovering over the button.

Did I really want to be plunged into darkness again—as an act of defiance? Maybe … I could just use it quickly to do some basic necessities: finding my own flashlights and some dry clothes, at the very least.

It's not like he'd ever *know* I used his lantern. And who cares if he did? Not me.

With that decision made, I grabbed the lantern off the

floor and padded to my bedroom at the end of the hall, determined to find my warmest clothes and maybe some spare blankets.

Once dressed in heavy layers, with an armload of heavy blankets, I decided to use the restroom, which still worked, thank goodness. I brushed my hair too and wiped off the smudged mascara, in case another visitor stopped by. Not Peter —because I didn't care what he thought of me. At all.

Before I left the room though, a memory crept in. One cold night before Christmas, Terry had regaled us with stories of living on his tree farm, which had included more than one story of electrical failures in the winter. When Mari had pragmatically asked him about water damage from burst pipes, he'd said something about leaving faucets on to prevent them from freezing. Was it worth trying? I might have remembered wrong. I decided it wouldn't hurt to let them drip just a bit.

I turned on the left dial for hot but then switched it off when I realized the heater wouldn't be working now. I'd let the cold side run. Or should I do both? I let out an agitated breath as I deliberated, finally turning on both before going to the kitchen to switch on those faucets as well. This was either the smartest or the stupidest thing I'd do today, probably.

While in the kitchen, I grabbed a few snacks and water bottles from the pantry and cast a worried look at the fridge, where I expected my food was starting to spoil.

Or would it stay cold since my house was becoming colder? I shook my head. I had no idea. Perhaps I wasn't cut out for being a homeowner.

I sighed, throwing the bags of chips and apples, along with the lantern, on the coffee table next to the couch. I was about to sink into the couch and pile on the blankets when I decided to check outside.

After moving the curtain aside, I gasped. The level of visibility was zero. Moving to the window closer to the front door, I gulped when the view confirmed it: these were whiteout conditions, and I was screwed.

I walked back over to the couch and flopped face down. Still chilled to the bone, I eventually rolled over and pulled the blankets around me, but it barely helped. I was still shaking—how long had I been shaking? At least I couldn't see my breath yet.

Could it get that cold in here?

Panic rose within me yet again as I fought to keep my breath steady.

I should turn off the lantern. It wasn't mine.

But I lay there frozen, though only figuratively … for now.

I thought about the inviting sights and sounds emanating from Peter's house, presumably the living room where a fireplace lit and warmed the room and calmed my senses with the satisfying crackling of wood and ashes.

My shivering, tired body screamed at me to swallow my pride. Go to his house.

Why did I let him get under my skin so much? I'd dealt with condescending jerks before, and it barely fazed me. But just thinking about that face—which was somehow arrogant and smug without even showing any discernible expression—had my blood boiling again. Not enough to warm myself though, unfortunately.

I almost laughed at the direction of my thoughts. An introvert I was not—neither was I a disaster-preparedness expert. I was living my worst nightmare.

I bit down on my lips hard. I tasted a bit of blood, though the pain was absent. My lips were becoming numb.

Would going to Peter's house and taking advantage of his questionable hospitality make things better or worse?

It was a lose-lose situation.

*****

When I knocked on Peter's door, he opened it without a word or even a smug expression. He merely stood to the side to let me enter and remove my snow-covered outer clothes and boots. I handed him the lantern, not daring to meet his eyes.

My body was exhausted from another trek through the storm with even deeper snow and a heavy overnight bag on my back, so I was grateful he didn't say a word. Maybe we could stay like this, just silently accommodating each other.

"I'm glad you finally came to your senses."

So much for blissful silence.

But I pressed my lips together and just nodded. I'd have to put up with his terrible attitude until the power came back on. I could do this. I'd done harder things in life. I'd dealt with many awful people in my career, oftentimes internet trolls who hated the pro-woman, body-positive, self-love content I posted online, but occasionally I met haters in person too. I had thick skin.

He waved me toward the room I'd spotted down the front hall, with warm light emanating from the doorway. "Come along."

We walked down the dim hallway on wood floors with a thick brown rug spanning the entire length of the hall. It felt soothing on my tired feet, and I wanted to stop and rest right here but kept plodding along slowly. Finally, we entered a moderate-sized sitting room. An enormous fireplace dominated the opposite wall, flanked by tall bookshelves. Two dark green sofas sat in the middle of the room, separated by a large oak coffee table. Stiff-backed chairs were arranged in a half-circle around a small, round glass table near the sizeable front window. And beneath our feet was a soft, richly woven rug that I suspected had a high price tag.

My body screamed at me to go sink into the couch nearest the fireplace and put my sore feet up. Instead, I merely dropped my bag on the floor and looked at him with raised eyebrows.

He scratched his head, looking slightly uncomfortable for the first time. "So, you'll be wanting to rest, I imagine. Are you hungry?" He sounded as though it pained him to ask me a question.

"Not really, I raided the snack shelf in my pantry before I left. Fortunately, I had a variety pack of corn chips that I bought a few weeks ago. Otherwise, there wasn't much left because …" Oh, crap, I couldn't tell him that I'd nearly run out of food because I was holed up in my house avoiding him. And why was I explaining anyway? "No, not hungry."

He nodded before pivoting on his heel and leaving the room.

I inhaled slowly, with an even slower exhale. He just *left* without a word. This man was maddening.

Then again, this was probably the best-case scenario. Being left alone in this cozy room without having to deal with him was better than I could've hoped, actually. But I frowned after scanning the room and seeing no blankets or even pillows.

Well, no matter. I could feel the heat from the fire already, so I'd make do without the comforts of sleep I was used to. I could handle anything except more cold and dark.

As I tried to find a comfortable position on the couch using my arms as a pillow, I heard his footsteps on the soft rug, and a few seconds later, a weight dropped on me. I yelped and scrambled to sit as I looked to see him hovering above me with his arms crossed.

I peered at the heavy heap. Blankets and a pillow. Two, actually. I almost smiled, as I always sleep with two pillows, but then he snatched one, along with a blanket, and placed them on the other couch.

Crap.

"Thanks. Are you, uh, planning to sleep here too?"

He nodded while stretching out his blanket, and I noticed for the first time that he was wearing sweatpants, plus the same T-shirt he'd been wearing earlier. How strange, as he didn't seem like the type of guy who owned sweatpants. Though admittedly I didn't know him that well, despite my instincts shouting that he was a pompous suit type who only wore silk pajamas, if he ever even slept, that is.

I must have been making a face, as he was looking at me with a raised eyebrow. "Something wrong?"

"Um … everything? What a hellish night." When he

continued eyeing me, I felt forced to add, "But thanks for letting me stay for a bit. I'll just … take a nap if you don't mind and then leave you in peace. I was going to try to stay out of your way while I'm here, but it appears you're staying in here?"

He exhaled slowly. "As you can see." Then he mumbled something I couldn't decipher while turning his back to me.

"What? I didn't catch that."

He sighed, turning around. "I said we need to conserve energy. The generator isn't supposed to power the whole house. My bedroom is toward the back of the house, so I was planning to sleep here anyway." His brows furrowed slightly. "Is that a problem?"

I winced. "Uh, no?" That sounded like a question. "No, it's not," I said, injecting more confidence in my voice than I felt. What did it matter, anyway? I'd be asleep soon, and hopefully by morning, the weather conditions and electricity outage would be resolved, so we'd have minimal chances to interact before I left.

But what if this wretched power cut isn't fixed by morning?
I refused to think about it.

The situation *had* to get better. It would.

Chapter 8

Before I even opened my eyes, I noticed the pressure on my abdomen. As I tried to sit and force my tired eyes open, the pressure shifted a bit.

Sleepy blue eyes looked back at me as a soft, furry tail tickled my cheek.

A Siamese cat was curled up on top of me. He opened his beautiful, soulful blue eyes and regarded me with faint interest. But when I raised my hand to pet him, he was gone in a flash. Not very trusting, I guess.

Wait, Peter had a cat?

No way. He couldn't possibly be an animal person, much less a cat person. Because I couldn't hate cat people. I was incapable.

He must be cat-sitting or something. For whom, I had no idea, since he probably didn't know anyone in Shipsvold. But it was the only possible explanation.

Closing my eyes, I tried to relax again, my body *finally* becoming warm and comfortable even though the sofa cushions were hard.

Before long, I sat up in frustration and rummaged around in my bag on the floor. Glancing over at Peter, I saw the tell-tale rise and fall of his chest and soft inhalations. I sighed, putting on my purple sleep cap.

I'd rarely told anyone I wore a hat to bed, much less let them see it. I'd learned long ago, freshman year of college in the dorms, that people thought it was weird. Beyond weird. I'd never met another soul who wore them, other than my late grandfather. But I didn't sleep well without my night cap. I'd even shooed men out of my bed before after doing the deed rather than letting them sleep over and going without my cap.

I slipped it on, hoping I'd awaken before Peter in the morning.

But if not, who cares? I didn't care what that man thought of me. And I doubted his opinion could sink any lower anyway.

I managed to fall asleep for a short time before waking again, more alert this time. I wondered if it was dawn yet. How would I even know if the wind was still whipping the snow in every direction?

I rolled over, this time without a cat in sight, and groaned.

Peter was gone, along with his blanket and pillow. He'd probably seen me with my silly night cap and—

Wait, nope. Don't care what he thinks.

Sitting up, I rubbed the sleep out of my eyes and placed my feet on the floor. I stood slowly and stretched my arms and back, which felt stiff because, well, I was a woman nearing thirty sleeping on a stiff couch. I padded over to the bay window and opened the velvet curtains using the string on the side.

My face fell. I couldn't see anything out this window. Snow or ice was stuck to almost every bit of the glass. I cursed under my breath as my shoulders sank.

Where was my nemesis-slash-reluctant host when I needed him? "Peter?" I called out, loudly cutting through the deafening silence.

He appeared within seconds, stopping a few feet in front of me and stuffing his hands in his pockets. He was wearing regular pants now, I noticed with disappointment. "Yes?"

"I believe 'good morning' is the customary greeting," I said irritably.

"Good morning," he said, his face its usual mask. "Sleep well?"

"Ah, well enough. I was wondering … what time is it?"

"It's almost ten."

My eyebrows shot up my forehead. "In the morning?"

He nodded. "Is that a problem?"

"I—" Stopping, I looked around. "I guess not. I mean, I had an important appointment today, but something tells me the roads won't be great for travel." My eyes met his again. "But I do need to get out of here. I hadn't planned on staying this late."

One dark eyebrow rose. "You think you're leaving?"

"I know I am," I said firmly, knowing nothing of the sort.

With my jaw set, I walked around him and down the hall to the front door. The rug was somehow dry, and my coat, hat, and scarf were hanging on silver hooks. I opened the heavy door and then proceeded to push the screen door open, but it wouldn't budge. I looked for a lock. Sighing in frustration, I turned back. He was standing right behind me with his arms crossed over his chest. I bit my lip, trying not to snap at him. "Can you unlock the door?"

"It's not locked." His face was blank, but there was something in his eyes. Amusement, maybe. Was he laughing at me?

"It is," I insisted. "I just tried to open—"

"It's the snow. Blocking the door," he said slowly as though he was speaking to a child.

Ugh, of course it would be the snow, trapping us in here together.

No. *No!*

"Well, do you have a shovel?" I asked desperately.

"Why?"

"So I can get out of your hair, obviously," I said through clenched teeth.

He shook his head. "Not necessary. Haven't you looked at the forecast?"

I narrowed my eyes. "You know I just woke up. And I don't have any devices with power; otherwise, I'd have—"

"Weatherman says it'll be colder and windier today, though the rate of snowfall will decrease later today." His tone was nonchalant, as though he weren't delivering devastating news. "And you still have no power."

I covered my face in my hands, wanting to scream but knowing it would do no good. "I might as well go back to sleep then."

He lifted his shoulders. "Suit yourself. I'll be in the kitchen."

I watched him as he walked down a different hall, his slippers making a clop-clop sound. I did a double-take. *Slippers?* He *so* didn't seem like a slippers type.

He halted, spinning around. "Did you say slippers?"

Crap, I said that aloud? "Uh, no. Just your imagination, dude." I made my best attempt at a smirk.

He raised an eyebrow but merely turned around, continuing on his way.

I shook my head at my awkwardness and padded back to the sitting room, where I gathered up the blankets and sank into the couch. Well, more like flopped onto the couch, since it wasn't the kind you sink into. See, *that* seemed more Peter-like. A firm couch. Not slippers and sweats. I chuckled. I must still be tired out of my mind.

As I lay with my eyes closed and my head warm in my cap though, the salty, savory smell of frying bacon assaulted my senses. I pulled the blanket over most of my face, trying to block it out. I couldn't believe the man actually cooked. Well, maybe it made sense since he didn't seem to have anyone else living here. But I imagined someone like him ordering from a fancy meal delivery service or a local fine dining place.

Then again, no one would be delivering in this weather. Perhaps this wasn't usually his thing.

Yes, that fit my vision of him better.

His food would probably not even taste good, since he didn't know what he was doing in the kitchen, most likely.

I definitely wasn't hungry. Not at all. I'd take a nice, long nap and then …

Bacon.

It was all I could think about.

Maybe eggs too.

But, *bacon*.

I couldn't handle it.

Absent any conscious decision, I found myself throwing off the covers and rising, following the scent down two hallways toward the only other room where I'd seen a light on.

I gasped when stepping into the room. The kitchen was only medium-sized, but it was one of the most beautiful I'd ever seen. It somehow blended an early twentieth-century aesthetic with contemporary appliances and fixtures, and the result should've been tacky, but it was anything but.

And in the center of it all, Peter looked up from the bread he'd been buttering on the massive kitchen island counter.

He had a plain black apron on, tied around his trim waist. His hair was a bit mussed, but not in a bad way—definitely not. And his full lips … they were glistening, with a tiny dab of purple near the corner.

Suddenly realizing I was staring, I blinked rapidly and pretended to check out the room before my eyes returned to his. Stepping forward, I pointed to the corner of my own mouth and then vaguely toward his. "You have a little something, right here."

He set down the butter knife and touched the right corner of his mouth.

"No, the other side." It was all I could do to avoid walking around the island to wipe it off for him. I watched him check the other side.

"Ah, is it gone now? Just some grape jam probably. I was sampling the food, sorry."

I opened my mouth, which remained suspended for a long moment before I closed it. "Uh, it's fine." Better than fine. "Maybe you're human after all."

I clamped my hand over my mouth and scrunched my face in an expression of epic regret. "Crap, I can't believe I just said that. I'm so sorry. Sometimes my, uh, my mouth moves faster than my inhibitions."

His eyes were glued to mine, and he just shook his head. "It's fine."

"What's fine?" I heard myself asking.

His brows furrowed slightly before he answered, "What you said, it's fine." With that, he returned his attention to the bread, and I watched him spread butter on a piece alongside another slice with jam.

"It looks delicious," I said. "Actually, it *smells* delicious, which is why I'm here. Do you mind if I … that is, if you have any leftovers, I'll take them. Or I could cook something for myself. I'm actually a great cook and an even better baker. But you already knew that, right?" I frowned. "Unless you didn't like my gift a couple weeks ago? If you froze the cookies, you must not have wanted to eat them all."

He let out a long sigh but didn't look up. I realized then I'd been rambling, as well as fishing for compliments. "I mean, it's OK either way. You know what, I'll just make myself—"

"Hazel, just relax. I made plenty of food for both of us. And your cookies were fine." He walked over to the stove to check on the eggs and then turned off the burner.

"Well, can I help at least?" I walked over and picked up the plate of bacon without waiting for his answer, which never came anyway.

After we both sat down to eat, I asked, "You don't talk much, do you?"

"I speak when necessary," he replied while stabbing scrambled eggs with a fork. "You talk a lot."

I licked some bacon grease off my lips, and I saw his eyes flick down for a millisecond. "I suppose I do, at least compared to you."

He shrugged and then took a long drink from his tall water glass.

Then he wiped his mouth and sat back, placing his elbows on the table and his hands together.

I bit into the fluffy, buttery bread and closed my eyes for a moment. "Wow, yum," I breathed. When I opened my eyes, he was staring at me without speaking. "You're surprisingly a great cook, Peter. The eggs and bacon are cooked to perfection. And this bread ... well, I'm guessing you didn't make it from scratch, but it's heavenly."

"I did make the bread. Thanks."

My mouth formed an *O*, but I merely nodded. "Wow, OK. I have to say ... you're not exactly what I expected."

"I probably shouldn't ask what you expected," he said warily as a lock of hair fell on his forehead.

"I ... yeah, you probably shouldn't," I said with a chuckle. After eating the last piece of bacon, my eyes swept over my empty plate and then his. "This was so good, but you've barely eaten anything."

He looked at his plate for a moment and then shrugged.

"Just not hungry? Or ..." I didn't want to try to speculate. I didn't like to comment on others' food habits as a rule, given that many of the women I met struggled with disordered eating—the last thing they needed was scrutiny from me. But it was odd that he'd cooked all this food but then only eaten a few bites.

"I had oatmeal earlier."

I made a face. "This is way better than oatmeal, Pete—er. Peter, I mean."

"It tastes better, sure." With a somewhat reluctant expression, he added, "But I can't eat this kind of stuff too often now."

"Why? Are you worried about your figure?" I laughed. This too was odd for me; I never asked or commented on people's body size or shape issues. But he brought out the worst in me, apparently. "Sorry, that was inappropriate."

His face was blank as usual. "Indeed. I'm just careful with my health now. My *figure* is fine."

More than fine, I'd say. He was trim but not in a skin-and-bones way. More of a lean muscled way. I had caught a glimpse of his stomach last night when he stretched his arms before bed and ... let's just say I agreed: his figure was nothing to worry about. "I guess if you're a health nut, that's probably why you didn't devour my cookies and brownies," I said, aiming for a casual tone.

"I'm not a health nut," he said briskly as his eyes narrowed. "Maybe you should stop assuming things about me."

I flinched. Crap, I've offended him. My host, who'd so far *not* been such a jerk this morning. "Peter, I—"

He looked down at my plate. "Well, it looks like we're both finished. I'll take your plate—"

"Oh no, I'll clean up. It's the least I can do," I offered, standing up to take my plate to the sink.

"There's no need."

"Well, you have a dishwasher anyway, so it'll be pretty easy—"

"I'm not running the dishwasher. Like I said before, we have to conserve."

"Oh, uh, I can wash them by hand though." I hated washing dishes and considered the dishwasher one of the best inventions ever. But I needed to earn my keep while I was here.

"No need. I'll do it. Just go back to the other room."

His tone was curt, and I stepped back quickly. "Oh. I'll get out of your way, sorry." He didn't respond as he filled up the sink with water. I turned to leave but then spun back around. "I forgot to ask. Do you by any chance have a cat? I could've sworn I woke up with a cat curled up on me during the night, but I haven't seen it since, so … I must have dreamed it?"

He turned off the faucet and glanced at me. "Yes, I have a cat. You're not likely to see him much though, as he's afraid of people."

"Oh, is he … did he have some kind of trauma?"

A dark look passed over his face then, but he hid it quickly by turning back to the sink. "Probably. Most of them do."

I wanted to ask what he meant by "most of them," but his tone suggested that the conversation was over, so I scurried away. With a sigh, I walked back to the sitting room. I'd give him a break from my awkward probing for now. Given the dismal weather forecast, I'd have plenty of time for intrusive questions later.

*****

My lashes fluttered as my lids opened just a fraction. As I slowly opened my eyes, the intricate design on the carved wooden ceiling came into view. As I studied it, the pattern almost seemed to come alive, with roses and stems swirling through one another. I shook my head and squeezed my eyes shut. I must still be half-asleep.

But a few minutes later, I was fully alert. I sprung up from the couch, my back feeling a bit achy from the position I'd slept in. I hadn't consciously decided on a nap, but reading one of the dull books found in Peter's library had lulled me to sleep. In fairness, they probably weren't Peter's books—they looked like they'd been here for at least a hundred years—and surely not *all* the books in here were dull. I loved to read and wouldn't be giving up after trying just one book.

After stretching my aching body, I looked around the room. I hadn't seen him since our late breakfast, which was fine by me, but as the clock on the mantel read almost 5 p.m., my stomach would probably start growling soon enough.

I should probably go find him.

I cringed at the thought, knowing another cutting remark and flat expression on his face would lead to another argument between us. I hated tension, and I was usually masterful at defusing it. He was just so difficult, more maddening than anyone I'd ever met. I wasn't even sure why, but there was just something about him. He rattled me.

It would probably be rude to help myself to things from his kitchen without asking, so I set out on a search. After all, it might be fun to wander about in an old home like this. I grabbed a flashlight from a basket he'd placed in the hallway.

Before I'd gone very far, I noticed a photo hanging on the wall leading to the kitchen. It was notable for being small but also being the *only* thing I'd seen hanging on the walls of this hall, other than some antique sconces. I peered at the photo closely but couldn't make out who was in the photo or what the inscription at the bottom said. It was a young boy with a middle-aged man, both smiling as the boy held up what looked like a trophy of some sort.

Could that be Peter? Possibly with his dad? The photo was too small and somewhat blurry, so I couldn't tell—plus, I had no idea what Peter looked like as a child, obviously. It must be important though if it was the *only* photo he'd hung up anywhere.

By the time I reached the kitchen, I'd found little more to examine apart from a large painting between two closed doors. The painting was a generic landscape with a plain stone path between wide, green fields bordered by old, uneven stone fences. It reminded me of the English countryside, and I could imagine Jane Austen walking merrily down the path with her sister, Cassandra.

Stepping into the kitchen at the end of the corridor, I found it empty, so I turned back and plodded down the same hallway. I'd have to try the other hallway, where he said his bedroom was and another room I couldn't remember.

This hall was similar to the other in that its only decoration was a series of ornately fashioned sconces. I paused at a few doors, unsure which was Peter's. When I'd passed four doors and still hadn't reached the end of the hall, I stopped and called out, "Hey, Peter?" After a beat, I knocked on one of the doors and then the next, adding loudly, "Are you in there?"

The silence was unsettling when I reached a stairway at the end of the hall. I didn't feel brave enough to wander farther in this dark, dusty, eerily quiet house by myself, so I turned around to head back.

But just as I turned, I screamed while slamming into a large, solid surface before I could raise my flashlight to see it. Hands grabbed my upper arms as I fought to shrink away and screamed again. When I'd finally wriggled to the floor and took off running after dropping the flashlight, I heard footsteps coming ever faster behind me.

My heart raced as I tried to run faster while being unable to see anything except the light from the sitting room down the hallway. "Peter! *Peter*! Help, please—"

"Hazel, what's gotten into you?" he growled, his voice seeming to come out of nowhere, and then suddenly he was beside me, his arm coming around my shoulders as we neared the soft light ahead.

I panted while glancing over at Peter, who wore an expression of concern, of fear even.

"Di-did you see it too? There was s-s-something back there. I … Peter, we have to—" I stammered while gripping his forearm, trying to pull him faster with me.

"Hazel, please. Calm down."

"*Calm down?*" I looked at him incredulously. "There's someone—"

He swung his hand around to grip my other shoulder and turned me to face him just outside the sitting room. "Hazel, breathe. Just try to breathe. Back there in the hallway, you ran into me. *Me*. We're the only two people in the house, I swear."

I blinked rapidly, trying to digest his words. "What?" With my mind racing, I shook my head. "No, I ran into something, and it grabbed me—"

"It was me," he repeated.

"But … they were really strong, with hands that—" My mind swirled, and I became aware of the gentle strength of his hands on my shoulders. "That was *you*?"

He nodded. "I told you, there's no one else in the house."

I swallowed. "But … why didn't you say anything? You scared the crap out of me!" I shrunk away from him, pushing back against his arms as my anger rose.

"You didn't exactly give me a chance. You were screaming and running before I could even utter a word."

I peered at his face, which spoke of exasperation but also relief, somehow. I swallowed again with some effort.

Turning away, I strode into the room and sank onto the

couch. I needed to catch my breath.

Although I didn't hear any footsteps this time, I could sense his presence beside the couch before I saw him. He sat on the other side of the couch, leaving at least two feet between us, and I was grateful for the distance.

I couldn't be upset with him. Thinking about his defense, he was right. I'd run straight into him; he'd probably tried to steady me so we didn't both fall over. Then I took off down the hall like a madwoman. And he'd tried to help me settle down.

Only something was still bothering me.

I was embarrassed.

But something else ...

My head swung in his direction. "OK, but where did you come from? I'd been calling your name, hearing nothing in response. Then suddenly you appeared, like a ghost."

For the briefest of moments, I thought he was going to laugh, as his lips twitched, but he covered his mouth with a hand. "Like a ghost? Really? Please don't tell me you believe in that nonsense."

I averted my eyes. "I mean, not really, but ... you have to admit, it was kind of creepy."

"I don't have to admit any such thing. But I see that you were frightened by my presence, and I apologize for that."

Wow, he was actually apologizing? Of all the things to apologize for, he picks *this*? I'm not even sure he did anything wrong.

Except ... where was he?

"But where were you? I was shouting your name."

"I guess if you were calling my name, I probably still had my headphones on."

I narrowed my eyes. "Why would you have headphones on?"

A muscle in his jaw tensed. "If you must know, I was working out. There's a room with fitness equipment in the middle of that hall."

I looked down at his clothes then, and sure enough, he was

wearing a blue T-shirt and workout shorts, along with athletic shoes. I exhaled loudly. "Well, OK. I feel like an idiot then."

He shook his head. "No need. I should've mentioned I'd be —"

"No, no. You don't owe me any explanation of what you're doing. We don't actually live together," I said with a nervous laugh. "It's fine … I've just been a little jumpy. To be honest, ever since this storm started, I've not been myself. I'm not really the type to be easily spooked, but I guess the combination of darkness and dead silence kind of freaks me out. Not to mention being trapped."

"Trapped?"

"Because of the blizzard."

He didn't reply, and we sat awkwardly for a few moments, both looking at the fireplace.

Finally, he cleared his throat. "So, I was thinking of making dinner—"

"Oh, no! Let me cook for us. It's the least I can do. That's actually the reason I was trying to find you, because I wanted to ask about making dinner." I bit my lip, thinking he'd probably never trust me in his kitchen now.

"That's not necessary. I can make a meal for us both. You should rest." His eyes swept over my face, probably seeing signs of worry or tiredness.

"I've spent all day resting, Peter. I'm good for now," I said with a small laugh. "Please, let me cook? I promise, I'm a good cook."

He looked like he was about to object, so I raised my hand between us. "Or maybe we can do it together?" He raised an eyebrow, and I continued, "I know you're not my biggest fan, especially now, but we should try to make the best of this situation."

His eyes held mine for a long moment, and I'd swear he wanted to ask something or maybe say something, but he simply nodded.

I smiled. "Thank you!" I realized this might be my first

genuine smile around him. When I giggled nervously for some reason, his eyes darted back to mine briefly as he walked alongside me.

But his legs were much longer, and his pace much faster, so I was trailing behind when he reached the kitchen. As I walked in, he already had a cutting board and knives on the counter. "Well, you work fast. What are we making?"

"I thought we could make a veggie stir fry if that's acceptable to you," he said, looking up briefly as he wiped down the counter thoroughly.

"That's fine. Great, actually. I'm starving." My eyes scanned the room. "Good thing you have a gas stove, right? No power needed for those. I wish I had one myself."

"It does need power, as the ignition is electric. But I have a generator, as you know."

"Oh, I understand." Though I didn't. "So, we can sauté some veggies and sauce and then cook some rice too?"

He nodded as he started chopping carrots and then waved toward another stack of produce. "Feel free to start prepping those."

"I usually put my produce in the fridge as soon as I get home, except bananas, even though I know a lot of produce doesn't require refrigeration. I don't know why I do it, but my parents always did growing up. But I'm glad you appear to not share in that habit, else we wouldn't have been able to enjoy these, am I right? Because you're trying to avoid opening the fridge and freezer to maintain a cold temperature in there, right?"

"Right," he said as he chopped.

"Sorry, I guess I talk too much."

"It's fine," he said nonchalantly while placing some scallions on the board.

After a long pause where I *tried* not to talk, I had to break the silence. It just felt weird to hear only the chopping sounds, amidst this ever-present tension between us.

"Would you by chance let me use your phone or other

device? I promise it'll be super quick. I just haven't been able to contact my agent at all since the power went out. I was supposed to meet with her today in the Cities. I mean, she's probably figured out by now, but—"

"It's fine."

"Oh, are you sure? You can even watch me type the message if you want to. I promise it'll be quick ..." I stopped, clamping a hand over my mouth before I could ramble some more. Ugh.

He turned to glance at me for a moment. If I didn't know better, I could swear his eyes held a trace of amusement. "I'm sure, Hazel."

After a long silence, I took a deep breath and said, "If I haven't said this already, thank you. I know we don't get along, like, at all, so it was kind of you to shelter me during the storm." I bit my lip, daring a glance upward at him.

"It's fine," he said again, not looking up this time.

"And sorry about earlier when I slammed into you and then screamed in your face. And everything after it."

"It's fine," he said, a bit more emphatically.

I sighed, realizing that's all I would get out of him.

Once we started cooking on the stove, I decided to try again. "So, are you a vegetarian?"

"No."

"Oh, I just thought ... you know, the veggie stir fry. Most rice dishes have meat."

"I enjoy meat, but I need to limit it."

"I suppose it's in the freezer too, which you don't want to open, so the cold doesn't escape. Hey, I just had an idea—we could use the snow outside as a freezer! I mean, we could literally transfer the stuff from your fridge and freezer into a snowbank or something."

Why did I keep talking incessantly? I didn't know, as I wasn't usually such a rambler.

He merely gave me a side-eye while stirring the veggies in the pan with oil.

"Or not," I said with a sigh. "Wait, did you say you *need* to limit meat? What's that about?" As soon as the questions were out of my mouth, I cringed. "I'm so sorry, that's a super intrusive question that I have no right to ask. I'll shut up now."

His expression blank, he turned to me. "I'm minimizing meat consumption for health reasons."

"Like general health, or a specific concern or … oh, crap! There I go again being intrusive. Just ignore me." My cheeks were surely flaming red by then. What was wrong with me tonight? I seemed to become a different, weird version of myself around this guy.

His phone timer went off then, and he checked the rice to see that it had drained. He then removed the veggies and sauce from the stove and placed it all on the island behind us. I watched, transfixed, as he fixed a plate for each of us. It seemed so odd that this guy could *cook*, of all things. But I wasn't complaining; rather, I was salivating as I sat down on one of the stools to eat. He sat on the stool next to me but edged away a bit.

I frowned. We'd just prepared dinner side by side, and now he was worried about sitting too close?

"I have heart arrhythmia and hypertension."

My eyes flared wide at his sudden admission. "Oh, uh, I'm sorry to hear that. Is it genetic, or does it have a more specific cause?" I looked at him as I chewed a large piece of broccoli. "It should go without saying at this point that you can choose to ignore any of my overly personal questions, by the way," I added in a self-deprecating tone.

"Both. It's caused by or worsened by stress. And there's a family history of stroke."

"Oh, sorry to hear that. Is it a distant relation like a grandparent, or—"

"My father and his father."

I nearly choked on a diced carrot and grabbed a glass of water to sip. "Wow, that's intense. I'm sure that's hard for you."

He nodded. "I have had to make a lot of changes."

I eyed him curiously, searching for some emotion, but

he was focused on his food. After several minutes of silence, I decided to go for broke and ask yet another question. "Does your recent move from Chicago have anything to do with this? The heart condition, that is."

He nodded simply and sipped some water. "Doctors said the stress of running a large company was going to kill me." He shook his head. "Ultimately my blood pressure readings for months in a row ended up being the deciding factor."

I listened with my eyes wide and focused on him as he opened up to me. I couldn't believe he was confiding all this, but it left a warm pang of something in my chest. "And Terry, he convinced you to move here?"

"Yes. For an easier pace of life." He sighed.

I studied his posture. He was uncomfortable, for sure. "You don't like it though."

His eyes swung over to me warily. "That's irrelevant."

"It's not irrelevant. Happiness is important. And you're clearly unhappy with your life change." I paused. "Were you happy before then?"

His hand paused in its path from his plate to his mouth, and then he set down his fork. "I suppose I thought so."

"Interesting."

"Is it?"

How could I explain that this version of him was a million times better than my prior one-dimensional view of him? "It's just, well, you have so many layers. I didn't know."

He held eye contact for a second and then looked back to his plate, which he pushed away. "It's not complicated."

"Oh." My voice was quiet, as his harsh tone clearly declared this conversation over.

Just as it was starting to become intriguing. As *he* was becoming intriguing.

Probably better this way though. We were not even friends. We were only forced together temporarily by unfortunate chance.

I needed to remember that.

Chapter 9

"Sofia, this is Hazel," I typed and then paused. "Hazel Tanaka-Katz. So sorry I missed our meeting today, but I'm stuck in a massive blizzard with no power. I'm using a friend's phone." I backspaced a few words. "A neighbor's phone. I'll call you when I'm back home with electricity."

I closed the messaging app and handed the phone back to Peter, who sat nearby in the other chair by the window after checking the situation outside, finding nothing but a wall of snow at the window. "Thank you. Man, I feel so bad about not showing up to meet with Sofia. And not even telling her. I don't know why I didn't think to ask for your phone earlier, so I could've contacted her already. She probably thinks I'm really irresponsible now."

He shook his head slightly. "Doubtful. If she's in or near the Twin Cities, she's in the same boat. They're getting masses of snow too, as they often do."

My eyes widened as my mind raced. "Oh, I didn't even—of course, that would make sense." My brows drew together then. "Well, now I'm worried about *her*."

He exhaled noisily. "I'll let you know if and when she responds."

"Oh, but don't you need to turn it off to save power?"

"It's in energy-saving mode right now, but I can enable text messaging."

"OK. Well, thank you so much … I really owe you."

His perfect brows furrowed for a moment. "No, you don't."

Amused, I glanced in his direction. "I beg to differ. But thank you nonetheless."

His eyes closed for a second, as though he was annoyed. "You can stop thanking me constantly. It's unnecessary."

I opened my mouth to disagree but then paused when I saw his determined expression. "All right. Maybe I'd better just stop talking altogether and stop annoying you." *Since you seem to dislike any type of conversation.*

He was silent and didn't look over at me.

"Well … maybe we can find something to do tonight before sleep. I'm not tired yet. Any ideas?" I bit my lip, surprised at my own words. I was essentially asking him to hang out with me—and why? We didn't like each other.

Because I was bored.

"I mean, you don't have to entertain me. I only thought that maybe you'd be a bit bored too and looking for a way to pass the time." But he didn't seem like the kind of guy who got bored easily; he seemed like the ultra-efficient and productive type. Maybe that was something he was trying to change though.

Ugh, why was I thinking about this? It didn't matter. He wasn't my friend or—anything else. We were just two neighbors stuck together in a crisis.

"I'll go get my tablet. Maybe we can watch a movie." He stood and left the room, and my jaw was nearly on the floor.

He wanted to watch a movie with me? I mean, it was perfect, a great way to pass the time. But also shocking, coming from him.

In a few minutes, he returned and sat on the couch. I rose from my chair and joined him on the couch, ensuring plenty of space between us.

As the device powered on, he turned to me. "Any ideas?"

"Well, I love rom-coms. Comedies too. The occasional drama. I hate horror. What do you like to watch?"

"Documentaries. Occasionally a mystery."

"Sorry, not a fan."

He scrolled on the tablet. "You can choose. What should I

look for?"

My smile was wide as I leaned over to take the tablet out of his hands. "I'll find something. There was this new release I wanted to see around Christmas but never got a chance … it's a rom-com about a couple that gets snowed in just before the holiday."

As soon as I said it, I realized the extreme awkwardness and ran my hand through my hair. "Oh, you know, maybe that would hit too close to home. I mean, we're not a couple, but the snowed-in part. I can try to think of something else if you—"

"It's fine, Hazel."

I bit my lip, peering at him. "Are you sure?"

"Load the movie," he said, sitting back against the cushions and crossing his arms over his chest.

As the movie started, I found myself leaning forward and sideways to see the screen on the coffee table. After a half hour or so, my neck started to ache, and my eyes were starting to hurt from squinting. I rubbed my neck and told Peter I needed to use the restroom.

Once there, I splashed water on my face and studied my face in the mirror. I looked tired. I suppose I was physically tired, but my mind felt very awake. My hair was thankfully still looking good, albeit a bit tousled. I was wearing a hoodie and leggings, the epitome of fashion.

Not that it mattered. I didn't care what Peter thought.

When I returned to the couch, he had grabbed two blankets, and I smiled gratefully as I settled into my corner of the couch and took the blanket he was holding out to me.

He shook his head though and waved his hand between us. "It's probably easier if we sit closer. I can hold the tablet so you don't have to crane your neck."

I moistened my lips as I felt my breath quicken, for reasons totally unclear. It wasn't like this meant *anything*. But he was being uncharacteristically nice, thinking about my needs. It was definitely attractive. Finally, I nodded and moved over, cutting the distance in half.

He furrowed his brows. "You'll need to come closer if you want to be comfortable. Squinting is bad for your eyes." At my nervous glance at the space between us, he added in an amused tone, "I'm not going to make a move on you."

"I-I wasn't worried about that."

And that was the truth. I knew he'd never make a move on me. He disliked me, a lot. Maybe hate was too strong a word, but he certainly wasn't interested in me either ... which was good. Because I had no interest in him.

None at all.

But I found it difficult to swallow as I closed the distance, leaving only two inches between us, at most. This was just weird because we didn't like each other and, well, I honestly couldn't remember the last time I curled up on the couch with a guy to watch a movie. At least three or four years, probably more. Although I'd had an active dating life before my recent break— OK, fine, maybe I *was* a serial dater—I rarely brought guys back to my apartment. I usually went home with the guy, not the other way around. And we weren't watching movies. That was more of a couple thing, which my dates had rarely progressed to.

Paying attention to the movie was difficult as I was concentrating so hard on trying to be casual about sitting close to him without actually touching him. It would be far more comfortable, physically at least, to lean against his side rather than to hold myself up rigidly beside him, but I had to avoid touching him. Otherwise, he'd likely recoil in horror, and I ... well, I didn't want to think about that.

Eventually, my attention shifted from this awkward situation to the one playing out on the screen. The parallels between the two were uncomfortable, to say the least, but eventually I got lost in the story, as per usual for romantic movies. When the couple in the movie tried unsuccessfully to dig the woman's car out of the snow and ended up buried in a snowbank themselves, I found myself laughing almost to the point of tears. As my laughs faded and the couple's antics on screen turned into an almost kiss, Peter made a noise. It sounded like laughter, but he must have been clearing his throat. I raised an eyebrow and quickly turned back to the small screen.

But I glanced at him every so often, and if I didn't know better, I'd almost say he was *enjoying* the movie. But that didn't seem possible because he was *so* not the romantic type. True to form, a look of disdain had crossed his face when I merely mentioned my love of rom-coms.

But then I saw it.

One corner of his mouth rose a bit and—wow, was he smiling? Almost smiling?

My eyes widened, and I must have made a sound because he turned to me with a questioning look.

"What?"

"I saw—never mind. Nothing," I said quickly, my eyes flickering between him and the tablet.

He raised an eyebrow but merely turned forward again toward the screen. Meanwhile, my gaze stayed on him. Studying his face, I noticed tiny fine lines between his brows, like many men our age, but I didn't see any lines around his mouth or eyes. I felt a pang in my chest when I realized what this meant: the man didn't smile often.

He turned to find me staring again, and I coughed and averted my eyes, though I knew I'd been caught.

"Are you all right, Hazel?"

"I'm fine. Ah—" I croaked. "I mean, it's a great movie, right? Sometimes I get emotional." And that was true, yet the man next to me was suddenly more riveting than this movie.

His forehead was creased as he gazed at me. "Can I get you some water? Or maybe a hot drink?"

I shook my head. "I'm fine," I managed to say.

No, no, I was not.

I didn't want him to start being nice.

He *could not* start being nice.

Because I could easily fall for a guy like that.

Chapter 10

As I stirred awake, I assumed my head slipped off my pillow because the surface beneath it was hard and unyielding.

But it was warm here, and the heavy blanket draped over my shoulder squeezed me like the coziest hug.

I moved my head again, trying to get more comfortable, and when that didn't work, I decided to tilt the pillow a bit.

"Oof!"

I froze, my eyes flying open and my brain trying valiantly to keep up. What on earth—where was I sleeping?

My hand was clasping a muscular thigh.

I was *using my neighbor's lap as a pillow.*

Oh no. Oh, I did *not* fall asleep on him. I started to push myself up and then covertly looked at his sweatpants to see if I'd left any drool there. Dry. Whew.

When I managed to get myself vertical, I backed away several inches as my eyes took him in.

He was rubbing his neck, and his heavy-lidded eyes slowly met mine. "Good morning," he said with a scratchy voice.

"Well, that's debatable," I muttered before putting on my best apologetic smile. "I am so, so sorry for whatever happened here. I'm assuming I just crashed after the movie? Or, wait, maybe it was *during.* I don't really remember anything from the documentary other than the beginning."

He nodded. "Yes, you fell asleep during the movie. I tried to wake you, but you just said, 'Goodnight, Pete' and then laid your head on my shoulder."

My face was on fire as I covered it with my hands and groaned. "Seriously, so sorry, Peter. I don't remember that at all. But this explains why my neck is so sore on the left side."

He nodded. "It's fine."

A new realization struck. "Oh my god, that means you had to sleep sitting up all night?"

He nodded again. "I don't think I slept much, but apparently some, as my neck hurts too."

I winced. "You should've tried harder to wake me. I feel terrible—"

"No, it's fine. Don't feel terrible." He yawned before saying gruffly, "You looked so peaceful."

"Well, that's nice, but I don't want to sleep peacefully at someone else's expense." I flashed a small smile then. "Even if that someone is you."

His mouth twitched. "Oh, really?"

"You're not that bad, actually." He was so close to a smile. I couldn't handle it if he did. He was already so gorgeous even when he was glaring or showing zero emotion. If he smiled, I'd have no chance. None. "I mean, you're OK *sometimes*."

He frowned, as though I'd hurt his feelings, but I knew that was next to impossible.

I cleared my throat and looked around for the water bottle I'd left on the coffee table. After taking a swig of it, I stretched my arms upward and rolled my neck a bit. "OK, well, let's see what our winter wonderland looks like this morning. I'll go look out the window if you want to check—"

"Already on it," he said while retrieving his phone from the table.

After looking out the window and seeing essentially the same view as the last two days, I sighed and turned back toward the couch where he still sat. "No change that I can see. Maybe we can look out the front door. Or do you have a back door?"

He didn't respond for a while, looking instead at his phone with a grimace. "The weather station says the snow has stopped in most areas, but the winds are even worse, so all the roads around here are closed. Near-zero visibility." He paused, swiping on his phone again several times. "And the power company gives the same old tired message." He exhaled deeply as he threw his phone on the couch beside him.

"Which is?"

"They're doing their best to restore power but have no estimate at this time." He shook his head. "The exact same message every time I've checked since this all started."

I frowned.

"Hazel, I'm sorry it's not better news." He looked genuinely sorry too, which was a first. As though the weather was his fault.

I shook my head and averted my eyes. Oddly, I wasn't frowning because of this news. I actually … didn't care. It didn't bother me that I'd be staying here a little longer.

And *that's* why I was frowning.

Because … what the heck? It's not like I wanted to stay.

"I will keep checking so we can find out as soon as things change."

I forced a smile. "No need to apologize for mother nature. It's not your fault. So, what shall we do today?"

"'We'?" he asked, his eyebrows raising slightly.

I felt like an idiot as I said quietly, "Sorry, I shouldn't assume you'd want to spend the day with me."

"I don't mind," he said, standing up to stretch. "I'm just surprised you want to. I stayed out of your way yesterday because … well, I thought you wanted that."

"I did." I laughed. "But then I changed my mind. You know, I've had far too much time to myself lately. I'm finding that I'm a little more extroverted than I thought. So maybe it's partly that."

He looked at me intently. "Do you want to talk about it?"

I shook my head.

"Well, let's get some breakfast. Do you mind dry cereal? I'm all out of eggs."

"It just so happens I love dry cereal." I grinned and followed him out of the room. "And I do mean completely dry.

Not even milk. I know, you probably think I'm a weirdo, like most people do."

When we reached the kitchen, he turned back to me. "You are an unusual woman. But not because of the dry cereal. I've tried to reduce dairy lately and have been surprised to find that dry cereal is delicious without milk too."

My cheeks warmed as I dwelled on his first sentence. He thought I was an unusual woman. In a good way or bad way? That could mean so many things. I wanted to ask, but—no, I shouldn't.

I didn't trust myself to respond appropriately regardless of his answer. "Just please tell me you have options besides plain cornflakes. That's the one cereal I can't abide. *Won't* abide."

"I'll see what I can find," he said, almost smiling. I had to look away, just in case ... *Quick, think of something else to talk about. Fast!*

"Hey, do you have board games?" I blurted. "That's a fun way to pass time."

"I have a few somewhere in the basement. We can go down there and look after we eat."

"I'm not sure why going into your probably dark, spooky basement sounds exciting, but it does." I laughed as we started eating our cereal at the kitchen island.

And then it happened.

His mouth curved upward on both sides, just a few millimeters, but it was enough.

I couldn't look away. Holy crap, his smile was stunning. He was beyond handsome. How was he still single?

His eyes suddenly blinked rapidly a few times, and he almost choked on his cereal. "Pardon?"

Oh no, had I said that aloud? "Uh, what? I didn't say anything."

"You asked how I was still single," he said slowly, his brow furrowed.

I avoided his eyes. "Well, no. I didn't say that," I lied.

"You didn't? What did you ask then?"

When I finally dared to look at him again, I saw amusement in his eyes, and I let out a sigh that may have sounded like a groan. "OK, maybe I did."

He pressed his lips together, as though trying not to laugh. "I'm single because I want to be."

"Oh, uh, OK." I played with my spoon a bit. "Not that I care. But why?"

He looked confused as he chewed. "Why what?"

"Why do you want to be single?"

He looked down at his cereal bowl for a long moment and then raised his eyes to meet mine. "I like being single. Only worrying about myself. The women I've dated—well, let's just say they were demanding. Selfish. Superficial. Undoubtedly, they wanted me for my money."

For some reason, when he referred to women from his past, I felt my stomach turn. "It sounds like you're terrible at picking women then. We're not all like that."

"Indeed. I've discovered that." He gazed at me then and swirled the water in his glass. "Some women wear old-fashioned sleeping caps."

I flushed. "Don't knock the night cap until you try it."

He put both hands up. "I wouldn't dare."

Needing a change of subject, I asked, "Are you almost finished? I'm dying to go see what board games you have. Let me guess—Monopoly?"

"Good guess. Yes, I actually collect different editions."

He said this with such a straight face that I couldn't stop a giggle from erupting. "Oh, that's so cute."

He narrowed his eyes. "How is it *cute*?"

"Well, it's—never mind. Let's just go, OK?" I hid my smile as I turned to put my bowl and spoon in the sink behind us.

I started to lead us out of the kitchen but then halted, and he almost ran into me. He stopped himself though with merely a brush of his chest against my back, and I nearly jumped out of my skin at the brief contact. "Ah, sorry. I'm, uh, sometimes I get jumpy. For no reason," I lied. "Anyway, I was just stopping to say

I have no idea where the basement door is, so you'll need to lead the way."

He brushed past me slightly, and I shivered. What was wrong with me? I was responding as though I was attracted to him, and I definitely wasn't.

Definitely not.

And even if I were, it wouldn't matter. He was *definitely* not into me. Or anyone, apparently.

I needed to get a grip.

*****

"You can't seriously be building more hotels."

Grinning, I placed two more little red buildings on the board. "Watch me."

"You are ruthless."

"Says you," I said with a laugh. "Aren't you, like, a finance nerd? Isn't real estate investing right up your alley?"

He crossed his arms over his chest. "It's not, because I run a greeting card company." His lips curved downward. "Well, I used to."

Greeting cards? That wasn't what I expected. For a fraction of a second, my mind wandered to Valentine's Day and how I'd be spending it alone this year. By choice, of course. Mari might be back by then, but she'd want to spend it with Terry. *And that's fine—I'm fine alone.*

My thoughts shifted to his last words. As he rolled the dice and progressed to a railroad he already owned, I eyed him curiously. "Are you bothered by that?"

He was still frowning when he raised his eyes to mine. "By what?"

"The past tense. Not running the company anymore, or any company."

He ran his hands over his lush brown hair, which my fingers ached to touch as well. Wait, what? Why was I thinking about touching his hair? I was *not* becoming smitten with this man.

Finally, after a long silence, he shook his head. "I

don't know if 'bothered' is the right word. It's certainly an adjustment."

"I mean, yeah, a massive one. It's a complete upheaval of your life, letting go of the fancy corporate job and moving to rural Minnesota."

He shrugged, but a muscle in his jaw tensed. Sensing he wasn't going to respond, I rolled the dice and moved my thimble to a utility he owned. "Ah, I don't have to pay rent, since you've mortgaged that one."

His frown somehow deepened as he looked down at the Monopoly board. Finally, he sat back in his chair and looked at me with narrowed eyes. "Not my best game."

"No?" I said, hiding a smile. "Let me guess, you're used to winning?"

He crossed his arms, his eyes not leaving mine. "Always."

"Why do I have a feeling you're not just talking about Monopoly?"

He scowled but said nothing, picking up the dice.

When I felt something brush against my ankle under the table, I gasped and nearly jumped out of my chair. He raised his eyes to my panicked face.

What was that? It wasn't Peter. "It was soft and furry, something slinking past me. Like—"

I watched as he bent down beneath the table and then surfaced with a cat in his arms. The same one I'd seen yesterday. Or maybe it was the day before? I'd lost track.

Closing my eyes in mortification, I sunk back into the chair and palmed my forehead. "Sorry, I should've known— I'm not usually this easily spooked, you know? It's this whole situation ..." I trailed off, realizing I was overexplaining. "Well, hello, kitty. Do you have a name?"

I actually loved cats. I wanted to pet this one, but I knew it was important to find out a cat's personality and preferences first. They could be very picky about people.

"This is Randy," he said as he rubbed the cat's cheeks. When I made a face, he sighed. "I know, kind of a weird name for a cat. But that's what somebody named it, and he won't answer to anything else."

I bit my lip to keep from laughing and oohing and ahhing. "I still can't believe you're a cat daddy. I never saw that coming."

His brows scrunched together as he looked down at the adorable cat, his blue eyes vibrant and as beautiful as his owner's eyes. "There are many things you don't know about me."

I nodded. "I'm learning that."

He tried to pick the cat fur off his pants but then gave up. "I don't even know why I try. He sheds worse than any other cat I've met, and he's a short hair!"

I wondered then how many other cats he'd known. And when he'd stop surprising me.

"So why haven't we seen more of Randy?"

"He can be skittish, especially around new people. And it's a big house ... he's still getting acclimated."

"May I pet him?"

The crease between his brows returned. "Well, you can try. But as I said, he's rather skittish most of the time. I'm surprised he came this close to you tonight."

I stood and walked slowly over to him as he eyed me with what I hoped was interest. "Nice to meet you, Randy. Can I pet you?" I held my hand out for him to sniff first and then raised it to the top of his head. But before I'd gone more than a few inches, I noticed the cower. He backed away, trying to huddle further into Peter's arms. Sensing alarm, Peter let him jump off and sprint away from us.

"Aww, I'm sorry I scared him. I'm usually pretty good with animals. Both cats and dogs love me, and I love them." I sighed while returning to my chair by the board. "Why do you think he's so skittish? Have you had him since he was young or—"

"No, he was a rescue," he said, a dark look passing over his features. "He was two years old when I adopted him last year."

I frowned. "Oh, so you think—"

"He didn't come from a good home," Peter said with gritted teeth. "Let's just leave it at that." He picked up the dice abruptly. "Is it my turn or yours?"

"I ... don't remember." I looked at the game board and then back up to his eyes. "Sorry for bringing up any past trauma. But if it matters, I'm glad Randy has you now."

I was glad? Why? Just a couple days ago, I didn't even like him enough to come to his house in an emergency, and now suddenly I thought he could be trusted with a helpless little animal? My head spun with the implications. Did I *like* him now? No, no, it couldn't go that far.

Peter's face relaxed a bit as he nodded. "Thank you. I just wish ..."

"What?"

He inhaled and exhaled slowly. "There are so many others in similar situations."

"And you wish you could do more?" I asked gently.

His lips were pressed together as he nodded, his mind seeming far off from where we were. A long moment later, his eyes met mine with something like ... wonder? Gratitude?

Or maybe shared struggle, as we were in this mess together. Maybe he decided he didn't quite hate me either.

I cleared my throat and pointed to the board. "You can take a turn now. The last one was mine." I had no idea, really, but I was afraid he'd shut down if we kept talking about this difficult subject.

His face showed relief as he rolled the dice. But then he grimaced, as he'd landed on Go to Jail.

Sensing that he was feeling sensitive, I resisted the urge to gloat. I tried, at least. But I was grinning as he looked at me with narrowed eyes.

"At least I'm safe from your expensive hotels and housing developments."

"For a turn."

"Or up to three turns."

"You should be so lucky."

I smiled then because, well, playing with him was *fun.* I hadn't had much fun in recent weeks and was glad to be enjoying myself. "If you're nice to me, I'll get you out of jail."

"How? The rules don't allow for that," he said, folding his arms on the table.

"Rules, schmules." I rolled my eyes. "I know how to break them and get away with it. The law degree has to pay off somehow, doesn't it?"

His eyes widened slightly before scrunching together. "You went to law school?" When I nodded, he asked, "I thought you were a motivational speaker or something?"

"I am. Or I was. I don't know anymore, actually," I admitted. "I'm taking a break to figure things out, write a book, and so on." I shrugged. "My legal career didn't last long."

"What happened?"

"I worked for a corporate law firm, and I loathed it. I was the *token woman*, the only person of color—and they made sure I never forgot it. Not like I ever could anyway. But aside from that, the ethics of it all, the blatant racism and sexism, the stifling expectations … I just couldn't do it anymore. I only lasted two years."

"Hmm," he said as he rolled doubles and then grimaced since he'd have to move out of jail and risk landing on my hotels. "You said you're going through a career shift now too?"

I was surprised at his sudden interest, but it was nice having someone to talk to. "I am. I'm tired of flying all over the country, sometimes outside the country, to meet and try to connect with people I'll likely never see again. I mean, it's great in many ways. I'm privileged to have done this for several years. But I'm just … tired. I want to stay in one place. For the first time in my life, I want to just be still."

I hadn't planned to say all that. And from the look on his face, he surely hadn't expected it either. But his tone was gentle as he replied, "For the first time in your life? Does that mean you've always traveled a lot?"

Sighing loudly, I looked down at the board, forgetting whose turn it was, and then returned my gaze to him. "I've travel extensively, yes, but I've also *lived* all over. My parents moved around when I was young, and then they split, so now I have to travel all over the world just to see them. And my sister." His expression was so focused on me that I felt bare, somehow. "We all live in different countries now, but Halley and I grew up in the States. Well, she ended up moving—it's a long story. Suffice it to say I'm not interested in the jet-setting life anymore. I want to settle. Finally, just settle somewhere. And who knows, maybe I'll hate it."

He nodded. "Maybe you will. But you have to try."

"Yes," I said. "You get it. Did you—was your childhood at all similar, or no?"

A shadow passed over his face, and his eyes darted down to the game board and then to the play money in front of him, which he proceeded to count. "I have $127, Hazel. You win. Let's be done."

I blinked rapidly and swallowed with real effort. He hadn't used that harsh tone all day. So we were back to that then? "I—OK, sure. Um, I'll clean up."

"No, I'll do it. You can go and …" He trailed off as we both realized I had nothing else to do. But sensing his mood, I backed away and turned to stride over to a bookcase on the opposite side of the room. Here was the only shelf of contemporary fiction; everything else was old.

As I ran my fingers lightly over the spines, I wondered if he'd bought them himself or received them as gifts. I'd already looked over every shelf several times in the past few days, but I never got tired of perusing his impressive collection.

My fingers stalled. Jane Austen's *Northanger Abbey* was right there, next to Elizabeth Gaskell's *North & South*. My lips curved into an excited smile before morphing into a frown.

I hadn't noticed the Austen book when I'd scanned these shelves before, and it would've caught my eye, as I was a major fan of her work—though the gothic-inspired *Northanger Abbey* wasn't my favorite. With a crease in my brows, I touched the spine reverently and shook my head. The book couldn't have been on the shelf before, as I would've surely noticed it. Had

Peter been reading it? That seemed highly unlikely.

Was this place haunted, like the abbey in the book?

I laughed at the silliness and then froze as my hair stood on end. Something or someone was behind me, close. I slowly turned my head.

I screamed. It was closer than I thought.

It was only *Peter*. Not a ghost.

But a ghost might've been better because ... wow, he was close. So close I felt his warm breath and had to bend my neck to meet his eyes, given our height difference.

Backing away a few inches, I tried to catch my breath. "Sorry—uh, I overreacted again. This house makes me jumpy for some reason."

He merely stared, his eyebrows slightly drawn together, and his hand twitched at his side.

Was he mad? Confused? Turned on? About to cry? I couldn't read him, and it rattled me. I couldn't stand the silence. "You have Jane Austen on your shelf? How is that possible?"

He raised an eyebrow almost imperceptibly but said nothing.

"I mean, it wasn't there yesterday. I swear it."

His lips parted, but still, he remained silent. I couldn't read him. At all.

"You're looking at me like ... I don't know," I said, uncertainty in my voice. "Like I'm crazy."

He shook his head, and his mouth twitched, almost as though he was about to laugh. "No. Not crazy."

His eyes seemed darker than usual, and he was leaning forward slightly. For a moment, I thought ...

No, he's not interested in me.

"I can't tell what you're thinking," I admitted softly. "Are you angry with me?"

"No."

"Well, what then?"

Finally, he tore his eyes away and looked past me at the bookshelf for a moment. "I came to—" His voice halted when his eyes returned to me. "To ..." His voice trailed off, and he shook his head briefly. "To focus. I mean, to apologize."

My eyes were wide as I stared back at this man who was clearly flustered, standing before me as though he'd forgotten why he had come. As though he'd forgotten his name. This hardly seemed like the Peter I'd come to know. "Are you all right?"

His lids were heavy as he slowly exhaled. "I don't know." He flexed his hand at his side. "No."

Now I *knew* I was crazy because his eyes—his whole posture—spoke of something I'd never seen from him, never wanted to see from him, and surely never thought I'd see.

Desire.

My heart pounded in my chest as I searched his face for clues. I must be misinterpreting because there's no way he ... he ...

The distance between us shortened as he leaned forward, or maybe I did—or we both did. My chest rose and fell with shallow breaths as I gazed at his slightly parted lips and then back up to his eyes, which were directed at my mouth. My fingers ached to reach out, to comb through his short, silky dark hair that was neatly cut yet less refined than usual tonight.

Suddenly I gripped his arms, but not in desire.

Fear.

A loud crash echoed in my ear, and I clung to him as my heart rate skyrocketed further.

"What was that?" I whispered, terror coursing through me.

He frowned, loosening my grip on his arms as his gaze cleared. "I don't—I don't know. But please, relax. It's probably just ... maybe something fell upstairs."

My eyes were wide as I fought to stay calm. "Re-relax? It could be—"

"Look, it's not like a bomb dropped on the house. I'm sure there's a reasonable explanation," he said, moving away as his brow furrowed in concentration. "I'll go look around."

"No, wait!" I said, grabbing his hand. When he stilled, I pleaded, "Don't leave me here alone."

He looked at me oddly and then nodded, taking my hand as he led me toward the back of the house through the hallway that had freaked me out before. I tried to take steady breaths as I followed his quick pace.

We reached the back door, and he started opening it with his other hand.

I tugged hard on his hand. "Wait! Are you insane? What if there's someone or something out there?"

He turned back, and our faces were close, too close. "Your imagination is working in overdrive. I think I know what made the sound." Then he turned and opened the door, looking out into the glittery snow that had finally stopped blowing enough that we could see more than a foot in front of us.

Sure enough, on one side of the house the snow was littered with dark debris, which looked like—

"See that? Looks like a large branch fell on the house. It happens sometimes when snow becomes too heavy and weakens the tree limb."

"A tree branch?" I asked, my tone incredulous.

He stuck his head out further and then stepped fully back into the house. "Looks like it only landed on the porch roof, so I'm guessing there was no damage to windows or anything. No power lines nearby."

I was speechless, which was incredibly rare. I concentrated on breathing, willing my heart rate to return to normal.

"It's all right, Hazel. Not a big deal—this kind of thing happens. It happened last week when it snowed, and that wasn't nearly as much snow as we have now." He even attempted a half-smile, which I was too distracted to fully appreciate. "I doubt there's any damage. We're safe." He grasped both my hands and looked into my eyes. "Are you all right?"

I nodded and then shook my head. "I—there's—"

"Breathe, Hazel."

Such simple advice, but coming from him, it was everything. I looked into his eyes before closing my own with a long sigh.

I backed away reluctantly. "I think ... I'll be OK. It's just been a long couple of days. I am not usually like this, you know. I'm usually cool, like ..."

"A cucumber?" He sucked in one cheek as if trying not to laugh.

I fought the urge to smile. To grab him by the shoulders and kiss him. Instead, I nodded slightly and attempted a more confident tone. "I'm fine."

I was definitely not fine.

*****

Our hands were still joined as we proceeded through a short walkway to the garage, which I assumed had once been detached since this was quite an old house. Thank goodness for twentieth-century innovations.

The garage was on the same side of the house where the branches appeared to have fallen. Once in the cold garage, he looked around, finding an LED lantern on a shelf by the door. After switching it on, he released my hand, and oddly, I felt disappointed.

He walked toward both sets of windows. "I don't see any sign of damage to the windows or elsewhere. This garage seems solidly built, so I think ..."

I stopped listening as my eyes landed on a large machine on one side of the garage, next to his car.

Was that ...

My eyebrows drew together as I squinted to read a label on it.

"Peter," I interrupted, pointing to the machine. "Isn't that a generator? I thought those had to be outside. And it's not connected to anything. I don't know a lot about generators, but don't they need to be hooked up to something? How ..." I looked at him for answers.

"The one we're using is outside, yes," he said, his tone impatient. "It's protected from the elements, as much as it can be. I've been checking on it once a day or so to make sure it's not getting wet or frozen."

My eyes traveled down to the machine and then back up at him a few times. "But … so what's this? An extra one?"

He nodded, as though that was obvious.

I opened my mouth and then closed it. Emotions swirled around within me at top speed, from shock to confusion to suspicion to annoyance …

Then *anger*.

I inhaled sharply through my nose. "So, you had an extra generator and *didn't think to tell me*?" I barely got the words out, with my voice shaking.

His expression changed, morphing into the blank one I'd seen the first couple of days with him. "That's right."

My eyes flared wide. "Why didn't you tell me?"

"Why would I?"

I scoffed. "Uh, because you could've lent it to me to use at *my* house instead of having me invade your space … why wouldn't you tell me this?"

He sighed. "You weren't invading anything."

"Then why? Did you—*do you* hate me that much that you wouldn't even lend it to me during emergency weather?"

"Hazel, let's go back to the fireplace where it's warmer. I'll get us a hot drink, a snack—"

"I don't want a *snack*, Peter. I'm not a child. I want answers. I want—" I stopped midsentence, unsure whether to continue.

Did I really want answers?

Maybe I didn't.

"Never mind. Fine, let's go inside. But I don't want anything from the damn kitchen. I just want to go to bed." I started striding past him, but he stopped me with a hand on my forearm.

"Hazel? It's simple. I—"

"I don't want to hear it," I snapped. His face changed then to one I hadn't seen before. Almost like sadness or regret. "At least not right now. Please, I'm tired."

He stared at me for a long time and then slowly let go of my arm. "OK. Let's go back."

Chapter 11

I awoke the next morning with my feet half-numb from Randy sitting on them and my forehead cold, as I'd forgotten to put on my sleep cap last night. I groaned, trying to bury myself deeper under the blanket, but then stifled a cry when it hurt to turn my neck. Great, neck problems too. Just what I needed.

After pulling my sleep cap off, I tried to smooth out my hair when I heard him rustling around on the other couch. I wondered why he hadn't just slept in his bedroom. I didn't know a lot about generators, but I assumed you could allocate energy to some things but not others—being able to sleep in a decently warm bedroom seemed like a priority.

Maybe he liked torturing me with his nearness.

Though with any luck, he would never know of my conflicted feelings. I *probably* just imagined that moment last night anyway. There's no way *that* guy was about to kiss me. I just haven't been myself lately, so my imagination was overactive.

I felt his eyes on me as I pulled the covers off fully and rose. Needing to get away, I dashed over to the front window, peeking behind the curtain. For the first time, the wind seemed to have settled down. And the beautiful, glittery white powder in every direction was a sight to see. I marveled at the beauty for a moment before frowning. Half the window was blocked by snow, and from what I could see, drifts were high in many places.

"I can't even see the mailboxes out there."

My body jolted as I spun around to face him. "Why are you always sneaking up on me?" I took several steps sideways, needing distance.

He leaned his shoulder against the wall next to the window. "I didn't realize I was. You scare easily."

I scowled. "No, I don't. Your house is just … creepy."

His mouth curved into a deep frown. "Creepy? I thought it a rather nice old house, or else I wouldn't have bought it."

I felt a pang of remorse. "Well, maybe it's nice when all the lights are on and the place is properly decorated. I wouldn't know, as the place has been vacant since before I moved in." Admittedly, I'd only lived here a few months, but he didn't need to know that.

He crossed his arms over his chest, and I tried not to stare at his biceps. "Well, I can't turn all the lights on. But I'm not sure what you mean about decorating."

"There's almost nothing on the walls. Hardly any framed photos, paintings, or anything else you'd expect to see in a big house." I paused. "I mean, I know you just moved here, but everything else seems to be unpacked and fully furnished." To be fair, I hadn't even seen most of the house; maybe he did all his best decorating in the other rooms I hadn't visited. That would be odd too though.

He shrugged. "So, I'm not into decorating. That makes my house creepy?"

"Well, that's not exactly—you know what, fine, it's not creepy." I sank into the chair nearest the window and buried my head in my hands. "Peter, I'm just … tired."

"Then go back to sleep."

I shook my head. "No. I'm tired of all this. It's been, what, three or four days? Five? I don't even know what day it is. I think it's cabin fever, and if I'm really honest, I was already struggling with that *before* the storm."

His head was slightly tilted as he replied, "You had cabin fever before we were snowed in?"

"That is what I said," I snapped. Shaking my head slowly, I buried my face in my hands again. "It doesn't matter. Just … can you check for updates on the outage?"

He nodded and pulled his phone out of his sweatpants pocket.

"You *sleep* with your phone in your pocket?"

"Yes," he said absently while looking down at said phone. "As CEO, I needed to be available at all times."

I stared at him for a moment as he swiped across the screen several times. "That sounds terrible. But you're not CEO anymore, right?"

He looked up briefly. "No. Old habit, I guess."

I shook my head to clear my thoughts. It didn't matter. I probably wouldn't see much of him after this whole ordeal; it's not like we were going to be friends. I needed to focus on getting out of here. Walking over to the window though, I felt demoralized because the snow looked so deep. Even if the power were restored, just making the hike in that much snow would be very difficult. It had to be three feet, or much higher in some places where the drifts were.

I turned around, wondering what was taking Peter so long. "Any news?"

"Yeah, it's just that the phone signal is a bit weak these past few days." His brow furrowed as his eyes swept back and forth across the screen. Then he put his phone in his pocket, looking thoughtful.

"Well? Don't keep me in suspense," I said as calmly as I could, trying to restrain my urge to shout.

His expression was blank as he delivered the news I'd been waiting for. "Estimated fix is this afternoon."

My eyes widened, and for the first time all day, I smiled, albeit only briefly. He didn't return the smile though. Instead, he dipped his head and then turned on his heel. I watched him walk away from me and then out of the room.

The infuriating man had just stomped away without a word! What the heck?

OK, he wasn't stomping. I was the one who felt like stomping. We should be celebrating—what the hell was his problem?

Feeling the irritation pumping through my veins, I turned back to the window. Maybe I should just go now. If power was being restored this afternoon, it wouldn't hurt to get home a bit before that.

The only problem is I'd be drenched and freezing. My boots were nowhere near high enough to keep me dry through all that snow, and I didn't have a snowsuit.

"I know what you're thinking. Don't."

I spun around, my heart in my throat. "Stop sneaking up on me!" I snapped.

He had the decency to nod as he said, "Sorry."

"And you don't know what I'm thinking," I mumbled.

He handed me a steaming mug. "Here, have some coffee and sit with me by the fire. We'll talk—"

I took the coffee from his hands. "I'll take the coffee, but I'll pass on the fireside chat."

I noticed how rigid his body was as he replied, "OK." His eyes bore into mine for a long time before he stuffed his hands in his pockets. "But you can't go."

My eyebrows slowly rose. "Oh, I can't?" I bit my lip. "What makes you think—"

"It's not just a matter of being cold and wet and uncomfortable as you walk over to your house, you know." I averted my eyes. Dammit, how did he know I was thinking that? "Once you get there, you'll be freezing with no heat and likely no hot water. And that's *if* you get there. You could get stuck."

"Stuck? You mean stuck here? I don't think you get to decide that—"

He sighed loudly and gripped my upper arms. His touch was gentle, but my skin was on fire where his fingers wrapped around. "I mean stuck in the snow. Unable to climb out. It looks very deep in some places."

I peeled his hands off my arms and stepped back. "Why

does it matter to you anyway?"

His face was stoic, in contrast to the fire in his eyes. He opened his mouth to reply before clamping it closed, his jaw muscles tensing. Finally, his usual mask of indifference returned. "Hazel, let's be rational."

My eyes flared wide as I digested his words. "That's it? That's your next move—calling me irrational?" I spit out, my hands on my hips and nails digging into my palm. "You are in no position—"

I went silent as a ringing sounded in the tense air around us.

Peter pressed his lips together and tore his eyes away as he took out his phone and brought it to his ear. "Yes?"

He nodded, and his jaw clenched as he stepped back a few inches, shooting me an intense look before turning away. "No, I don't." What followed was a series of similarly short, abrupt answers.

Finally, he lowered the phone from his ear and turned toward me, his facial muscles relaxed even while his eyes narrowed. "They want to video chat with you. I don't know if the signal is strong enough, but you can try."

"They ... who?" Then, realization dawned. "Is that Mari?"

He nodded, holding out the phone to me.

I was careful not to brush against his fingers as I took the phone from him. I needed distance, more than ever. I pressed the video button on the screen and waited for it to load. "Mari? Can you hear me?"

"Yes! Hazel, I've missed you. Are you all right? I've been trying to call you and was terrified something had happened to you!"

Finally, my best friend's beautiful yet distressed face filled the screen. My smile was genuine as I nodded. "I'm fine, more or less. We've been having the blizzard that never ends. Today's the first day I can see *anything* out the window. I haven't been outside in days ... but I'm fine. How are you?"

Mariana's brows furrowed. "We're fine, other than being

worried about you. We had to postpone our return flight since we were supposed to fly out tonight, but the MSP airport is still closed."

"Oh, I didn't realize you were supposed to return today. That's a bummer that you can't though."

She squinted. "Your video feed is a bit blurry. But yeah, don't you remember? I told you I got a great deal on a return flight on Valentine's Day. You joked about the Mile High Club, and then we—" She paused, her mouth curving downward. "Are you all right, Haz? Did I say something?"

The blood was draining from my face as the news sunk in.

It was Valentine's Day.

Today.

And I was stuck here with the most infuriating man on earth.

I shook my head, trying to smile as I caught my breath. "No, I'm fine. I'm just—I forgot about the holiday." I forced my smile to widen. "I hope you two are celebrating since the flight is delayed."

Mariana stared at me for a long moment. "Oh, I get it. Oh, no, Hazel, I feel so bad. You're snowed in on *Valentine's Day*. The favorite day of all romantics. You must be devastated. I'm so sorry—"

I cut in before she could embarrass me anymore. "No, I don't care about that. I'm taking a break from dating, remember? I couldn't care less about a holiday for lovers," I lied, careful to smile brightly to prove I didn't care.

"But you've always *loved* this day. Once, you even said—"

"Mari, can we just drop it? It's not a big deal. Especially in this literal weather emergency ..." I trailed off, giving her another forced smile.

"Oh, but you're not alone! I almost forgot—Terry said you're staying with Peter. He lives next door? How perfect!"

"I don't know about 'perfect,' but he let me stay here since he has power and I don't. I'm using his phone."

"That's so kind of him. I'm happy to see you guys are

becoming friends now. It would've been a little awkward if—"

"We're not. Friends, I mean. We still don't like each other."

Mariana's face fell. "Oh. Well—oh, hi, Peter!"

My eyes widened as I turned to see him behind me, apparently visible on camera. "What did I say about sneaking up on me?" I hissed.

He ignored me and looked at the small screen with his usual bland expression. "Hi, Mariana. I hope you're doing well."

She grinned at him. "I am, though our flight back is delayed. Thank you so much for taking care of my best friend during this storm. It sounds awful!"

He nodded and then turned to me. "Hazel, I just wanted to see if you were hungry for breakfast yet."

Still fuming, I turned to him and whispered, "I'll find something to eat myself when I'm done."

His eyes lingered on my face a little too long before he walked away. Admittedly, I wouldn't have noticed if I hadn't been looking at him too.

When I turned to look at the screen, Mariana's lips were curved into a frown, and her forehead was creased. "So, you're not getting along?" It was a question, but she said it like a statement.

I sighed. "Sometimes. But not today."

"And you're stuck spending Valentine's Day with him."

I grimaced. "OK, enough about Valentine's Day. I don't want to talk about it." Hearing a noise, I looked sideways, and sure enough, he was still in the room, tidying up around the sofas. Seriously? I clenched my teeth as I forced another smile. "But I want to hear about your honeymoon. I mean, it's Italy! I need to hear everything."

Mariana looked at me warily for an extra beat before smiling reluctantly. "And I look forward to catching up, but your picture is blurry and you're not using your own phone, so ... we should connect again when I'm back."

I nodded. "You're right ... just missing you. Pinecone too. I'm going insane here." Sighing, I raised my hand in a small wave. "Bye, Mari. Call me when you get back!"

Fortunately, Peter had finally gone, so I padded over to the couch and set the phone on the coffee table. I grabbed the thick blanket that he'd carefully folded and tossed it over me as I lay down.

I might as well nap. With any luck, the power would be restored when I awakened.

This afternoon couldn't come soon enough.

*****

After lying awake for an hour hearing my stomach growling, I finally dragged myself off the couch. I wasn't the sort of person who could sleep while ravenous. Was anyone that sort of person? I couldn't imagine it.

I grabbed my overnight bag, which had, naturally, been woefully inadequate for more than one night. I was wearing the same leggings and long-sleeve shirt from yesterday, and I'd packed no makeup, only a few hygiene essentials. I hadn't freshened up since the second day of my stay here. Yesterday, hoping to be able to go home, I had put off bathing. I sighed as I walked to the bathroom just down the hall, deliberating on whether I should shower or wait until I got home.

But what if my pipes were frozen or the hot water heater took a long time to start working again—or any number of other technical failures I didn't want to imagine? I grimaced as I pushed the bathroom door open.

And for the thousandth time since I'd arrived here, I screamed. The unlocked bathroom door had caused me to assume it was unoccupied, which is a normal assumption, right?

But there he was, wearing only a towel wrapped around his waist, with his wet hair slightly dripping on his face and his chest.

Holy … his chest … oh no.

No, no, no!

I did *not* need to see this.

Against my will, my eyes drank him in. I wouldn't have expected a stuffy CEO workaholic to have a six-pack … or sculpted shoulders like that. Every inch of him was firm, muscular, lean without being bulky. I shouldn't be surprised, as I'd seen hints of biceps when he wore a short-sleeve shirt to bed or when I'd seen his calves in his sleep shorts. Of course, he hadn't worn shorts again since that first day.

I needed to stop *now*. My hands flew up to cover my eyes.

"I—you—" My voice sounded like a squeal. "Don't you lock the doors when you shower?"

His voice held a note of amusement. "Not usually. I live alone."

"But—but—" I sputtered. "Not right now you don't. I'm still here, or did you forget?"

"No, I definitely didn't forget." A trace of a smirk graced his lips.

And I knew then that I'd been caught.

How long had I ogled him? He must have watched me watching him. I took a deep breath and raised my chin, attempting a neutral, unaffected expression. "Whatever. I'll go grab breakfast, and hopefully you'll be done by then."

He pressed his lips together. Was he trying not to laugh at me? I almost wished he would, so I could see his face transform—

No!

Stop thinking like that, Hazel.

You don't like him, and he doesn't like you. Period.

Before I could humiliate myself further, I darted out of the room and speed-walked to the kitchen.

While making a small salad, I'd almost convinced myself everything was fine—great, even, since I was going home. And then I remembered.

It's Valentine's Day.

And I couldn't pass it off as not caring about the stupid holiday, because Peter overheard more than I cared to remember from that video call.

Ugh, it was a whole new level of awkwardness, and that was *before* I walked in on him wearing only a towel.

*****

Each hour that passed, my hopes deflated a bit more, and by dinnertime, I felt defeated. I'd be stuck here for another night, at least. With that in mind, I accepted Peter's offer to cook and wandered down to the kitchen at the suggested time.

Laid out on the kitchen island was a buffet of muffins, salami, and nonperishable foods, and I felt the rumbling in my stomach as my eyes flew to his.

"Is this adequate?" he asked with a completely straight face.

I bit my lip, trying not to smile. "I'm still mad at you for the generator thing," I said while pulling out the stool to sit. "But I'm not going to lie: this is a great way to start making amends." I offered an overly sweet smile before grabbing a muffin.

Delicious chocolatey banana goodness exploded in my mouth. "What kind of muffins are these?"

He finished chewing a blueberry and replied, "Banana and chocolate."

I rolled my eyes. "Well, of course, but what kind? Like, what brand? They're to die for, and I want to buy my own."

"You won't find them in a store."

"Why—" I stopped, looking at him closely. He was avoiding my eyes. "Did you *make* these yourself?"

He nodded, popping two more blueberries in his mouth, and I tried not to stare at his lips.

"Wow. I thought I was the baking queen of Shipsvold, or at least this neighborhood." I laughed. "I might have to give up my crown though. These are amazing."

"Thank you. I'm glad you're enjoying them," he said quietly.

We ate silently for a few minutes until I couldn't stand the silence any longer. We seemed to have reached an uneasy peace now, and though I wasn't eager to put that at risk, I'd had enough of the stifling silence of recent days to last me a lifetime.

"Tell me more about your heart condition."

His gaze traveled from his plate to my face and then back down to his food. He stuffed another forkful of bran cereal in his mouth. Finally, he turned to me with his fork down. "What do you want to know?"

"Sorry if it sounds intrusive, but ..." I paused, waving my hand around. "This whole situation is so bizarre; I figured the question isn't *that* out of bounds. After all, you're not only my new neighbor but also a close friend of my best friend's husband. Wow, that is a mouthful."

His eyes flickered down for a moment and then returned to stare at me. "Ask whatever you want."

"Well, what did the doctors say? How are you doing? How'd you know you had the condition?"

He took his time drinking from his water glass. "It became hard to ignore the palpitations, though I tried. Then one day I fainted, so I went to a cardiologist, who said I can manage the condition with some lifestyle changes. Relatively standard advice for heart health. Sleep more, exercise but not too hard, eat healthy, reduce stress, quit my job."

"Wow. Most of that sounds reasonable, but I don't think quitting your job is standard medical advice. Your job must have been super stressful."

He shrugged. "It was all I knew. I was thriving."

"Or so you thought."

He slowly nodded. "Or so I thought."

I shook my head in wonder. "I've considered my job stressful at times—I mean, who hasn't? But never to that level." I paused. "Though I do know someone who had to quit her job in the mental health field because it became too much. She's now my assistant—well, she's actually an event coordinator at the resort, but she does part-time work for me too. In fact, she set up —" I halted, the blood draining from my face.

"What did she set up?" His eyebrows lifted. "What's

wrong, Hazel?"

I smacked my forehead. "Dammit, I am such a jerk." At his look of confusion, I explained, "It *just* occurred to me that I never messaged Roxy. I sent my agent a message from your phone the other day, but I forgot to contact Roxy. Oh, I hope she's OK. Would you mind—" I stopped when he started to hand me his phone, and I smiled. "Thank you."

"You're welcome. But who is Roxy?"

"My assistant—she sets up my events and meetings, including the one I missed the first day of the blizzard. Oh, man, I hope Sofia let her know." I widened my eyes. "What if Roxy's in trouble? I hope she's somewhere warm … then again, I think she lives downtown, so perhaps they have done some plowing there. Or maybe there's a warm place to stay in town. Sometimes I wish I didn't live so far on the edge of town. Though sometimes it's nice too."

One of his cheeks dimpled slightly as the corner of his mouth lifted. "Got it. So, are you going to message her?"

It was only a half-smile, a crooked one at that—but he was easily the most striking man I'd met in a long time. Maybe ever.

I swallowed with serious effort and bit my lip, wincing when it hurt.

His barely-there smile vanished. "Hazel?"

"Oh, uh, right. I'm going to text Roxy."

He nodded and crossed his arms over his hard chest, which I had to tear my eyes away from.

It must be the cabin fever. I could barely think around him. Thank goodness he wasn't smiling anymore. And rarely did.

As I texted Roxy, a cacophony of machines suddenly arose, and the bright overhead light flickered. I looked around with anticipation, waiting to see if they stayed on.

The lights and machines were alive again, signaling the power was restored. I turned and flashed Peter a wide smile, squeezing his hand as I bounced a few times on the stool.

"Come on," I said, tugging on his hand as I stood up. He

resisted the pull though. "Dance with me!"

He shook his head, his lips twitching. "No thanks. I don't dance, and there's no music."

I laughed at him while twirling around. "No music? Can't you hear that? It's the most beautiful sound I've ever heard."

He was watching my every move with an expression I didn't recognize, and I didn't even care. Finally, he spoke, "I've never thought of electricity as beautiful."

"Me neither, actually," I said, smiling at everything around me as I danced. After a few minutes, I plopped back onto the stool and chugged the rest of my glass of lukewarm water. "Come on, let's hurry and clean up so I can go pack!" I giggled. "Not that I have much to pack though. I never thought I'd be here so long."

His face hardened as he rose. "Well, there's no rush. You'll be here at least another day. You can't go home tonight." And with that odd statement, he turned his back and started tidying up.

I gasped, clutching the chair to keep me steady as I processed this incomprehensible statement ... no, this *declaration.*

"What—why not? You think you can decide for me?" I asked incredulously. When he didn't turn or speak, I spoke more loudly. "Peter? What the heck? Please tell me you're joking."

His head swiveled around. "I don't joke about matters of safety. It's not wise to leave yet," he said, his tone harsh.

"But why?" I shook my head, dumbfounded. Why was he acting like this? "You know what, it doesn't matter. No one else makes decisions for me. Certainly not *you.*"

His lips were pressed in a thin line. "Someone has to make the rational decisions."

"Now you're accusing me of being irrational again? What on earth gives you the right—"

"Hazel," he said firmly, putting his hands up at the level of his chest. "I don't want to argue. Let's just clean up and get ready for bed—"

My eyes were wide as I scoffed. "I'm not going to bed with you!"

He sighed, frustration seeping out of every pore. "You know that's not what I meant."

"I don't know what you're trying to say, but let me just say this again. *You can't decide for me.*" I swallowed a couple times. "I'm leaving. And that's final."

He shook his head and stared at me. "No."

"Yes, I am," I said while stomping out of the kitchen. I practically ran down the long hall to the sitting room, barely noticing the fact that everything looked quite different—that is, not creepy—with more lights on and the familiar whirr of devices.

A minute or two later though, he appeared in the room as I was kneeling on the floor by my bag. "Hazel, please."

I inhaled and exhaled slowly. "Just stop. I don't want to argue with you."

"I don't want to argue either. I—" He paused, his eyes uncertain but holding contact with mine. "I'm sorry."

My face softened a bit. It was strange hearing an apology from him, and I guessed he did so only rarely. I nodded before throwing my sleep cap and extra socks back in my bag. "Have you seen my slippers? I thought they were over here by the couch, but I'm not seeing them."

He shook his head. "Don't worry about it. We'll find them tomorrow."

My eyes snapped to his. "Why would I come back here tomorrow?"

His eyes narrowed to slits, and a muscle in his jaw tightened.

"Are you serious? You still think I'm staying here?" I accused, marching up to him with a scowl.

When we were almost eye to eye, he inhaled sharply but blew out his breath slowly. "It's not safe," he ground out, his teeth still clenched.

My face was hot with rage as I pressed my lips together

before opening my mouth to speak. But the words wouldn't come, and we just stared at one another, anger thick in the air.

Finally, I exhaled loudly. "Don't you *want* me to leave?"

His eyes held mine with an intensity that shocked me. "No," he barked.

I blinked rapidly as my eyebrows scrunched together. "What—I don't get it. *Why not?*" I stopped to catch my breath. "I'm doing you a favor by leaving. Why are you being so stubborn and … I don't know, is this you being overprotective?"

His face was stoic as I stared at him, waiting for him to say something—anything—that made sense.

"You know what? It doesn't matter. You can disagree with me, but you can't stop me. I'm going."

He just glared back at me, not moving a muscle.

"I just have to get a couple things from the bathroom, and then I'm leaving." I waited for a response or even some indication that he *might* respond but found none. Tearing my eyes away, I turned on my heel, bent down to grab my bag, and walked as calmly as I could to the bathroom.

My heart was racing, and I felt torn between wanting to scream and wanting to cry. I couldn't remember the last time I'd been this emotional. Scanning the bathroom counter, I tried to breathe steadily as I found the few toiletries and a toothbrush I'd brought and then stuffed them into my bag.

"Goodbye, Peter. Thanks for letting me hang out here," I called out from the hallway, not bothering to stick my head in the room where he stood, stock still. There was no point. But I could at least be polite.

Reaching the front door, I saw that my coat and snow gear were dry, clean, and laid neatly on a broad chair. Well, at least he was thoughtful. Once I was bundled up as best I could, with my bag over my shoulders, I took a deep breath and tried to mentally prepare for the trek back home.

Finally, I opened the door and was immediately struck with the beauty of the glistening white landscape that lit up the night. I marveled at how something so disastrous and potentially destructive could produce something so utterly beautiful. Before I could ponder further, I took a deep breath and stepped outside, glancing behind me just briefly as I took hold of the door.

He was there, a small figure much further down the hall, but I knew he was watching me. I shivered, darting off into the cold.

Chapter 12

Amazingly, the dripping faucet trick worked. The pipes didn't freeze. And I was reaping the benefits now as every part of my body submerged in the bath was cooing with delight. The heat was seeping into my bones, into my soul.

I'd have to make sure I didn't fall asleep in the tub.

It was the best bathtub I'd ever experienced, and I'd had the pleasure of many different kinds of bathing experiences, given the extensive traveling I'd done. When I became a homeowner, this room had a boring modern shower and small tub, but I'd splurged on a contractor to rip it all out and install this lavish clawfoot tub.

With a lazy yawn, I was reaching for the loofah when the bell rang out.

I stilled. It was my doorbell. Who would be ringing at this hour? As far as I'd seen on my harrowing walk to my house, the roads didn't look even remotely passable. It could only be …

Peter.

I squeezed my eyes shut, willing the visitor to go away.

Or maybe Doris, the retiree down the road, had come back from her trip early?

Unlikely.

I'd just ignore it. Whoever it was—well, it had to be Peter—would go away if I didn't answer.

I sank back into the water, sighing as the steam felt cleansing in more ways than one.

My relaxation was once again cut short though as the bell sounded again. I grimaced, deciding to ignore it. I wish I had earplugs in here.

The bell sounded again a minute later and again in half that time; the sounds were coming closer together, as though the visitor were becoming impatient.

Well, he can be as impatient as he wants to be. I'm not giving him the satisfaction—

Ring. Ring. Ring.

OK, now he was pressing it repeatedly, and I thought I heard pounding as well.

Sinking into the water further, I groaned.

This wasn't going to work. How could I forget: the man was even more stubborn than I was.

Swearing profusely, I accepted the inevitable. I'd get out of the bath to answer the door, yell at him, and then come back to the bath, maybe adding some more hot water and bubbles. Then I'd grab my coziest pajamas and some hot cocoa before going to sleep. I smiled, thinking of the bliss I'd soon be experiencing. Assuming I could get him to leave.

I frowned.

That might be easier said than done.

The bell was ringing even more frequently now, and the knocking was almost continuous.

Sighing, I forced myself to get out of the warm haven, which was quite possibly the hardest thing I'd done all week, even worse than the blizzard walks. Since I had every intention of coming straight back to my bath, I quickly toweled off, grabbed my pink robe from the hook, and wrapped myself up.

Under ordinary circumstances, of course, I wouldn't answer my front door in a bathrobe. But Peter and I had been in pretty close quarters for days, so it wasn't a big deal. The likelihood of the caller being anyone else was miniscule.

After opening the door, I stood in front of it to block his entrance. "Peter. What are you doing here?"

I was wrong. It was a big deal.

His eyes widened and then went hazy as they slowly swept downward, lingering on each of my ample curves, and then moved even more slowly back up to my face. His hand twitched at his side. His lips were dark pink from the cold and parted as though he was going to speak or … something else.

I put my hands on my hips, impatient to end this interaction, but only too soon discovered that was a bad idea, as his eyes once again flickered down.

He seemed shocked that I'd answered the door this way. Disdainful, maybe.

He was *not* mesmerized by my robe-clad body. He couldn't be, because he didn't even like me.

After clearing his throat, he swallowed. "Let me in, Hazel."

My eyes flared with indignation. "Why?"

"Just let me in."

Crossing my arms over my chest, I said, "No."

He looked away for a moment and closed his eyes slowly before refocusing on me. "I'm obviously not leaving you alone."

With my eyes widened, I fumbled for words. "Huh? You … why not?"

"I think you know why."

My eyes narrowed. "I don't."

Before I could respond or even take a breath, he closed the distance in a second and wrapped his arms around my shoulders, his fingers threading up through my damp hair. Before I could process the shocking feel of his hands on me, his lips urgently descended on mine. I gasped against his mouth, and he gently pulled back so that his burning eyes met mine.

I shivered from head to toe and tried to form words. But I couldn't even form a thought, much less actual words.

When I swallowed and licked my lips, his fiery gaze settled on my mouth before he leaned in painfully slowly, and I was vaguely aware of my hands gripping his solid upper arms as our lips met again. I leaned in, sliding my hands up to his thick shoulders to pull him toward me.

His hands were gentle on my cheeks, and he kept the kiss

slow, tender, exploratory. But I wanted the urgency, the frantic rush, so I could lose myself in this …

Somewhere from beyond the heady feeling I'd succumbed to so easily came a voice, a whisper only.

What are you doing?

My awareness rising, I tore my lips away from his and pushed back against his chest before stepping back. I put my hand on my own chest, trying to catch my breath, with my eyes wildly searching his face, taking in the raw passion in his already handsome face as he gazed at me with heavy lids.

Still panting, I sputtered, "What—what the hell was that?"

His eyes became clearer as his face settled into a frown. "What?"

Isn't the question obvious?

"Why did you kiss me?" I demanded, tugging on my robe strings to confirm they were still tied tightly.

He merely shrugged and strode over to my couch. And then he sat down.

The man just kissed me senseless out of *nowhere*, and now he was going to sit down and make himself at home?

What alternate universe was this?

When he merely gazed at me from the couch, I shook my head in confusion. "What are you doing here anyway? You can't just … march in here and demand to stay."

"I can't?" He shrugged. "Well, I just did."

I gasped. "Well, the answer is no. You—you need to go. I need … space." My fingers touched my lips absently. "I don't understand what just happened."

"You're overthinking," he said while leaning back against the sofa cushion.

I scoffed. "You're *underthinking*."

He sighed and crossed his legs at the ankles while saying nothing. When did he take his boots off? I didn't even notice.

And why was he getting comfortable on my couch?

What just happened?

I sat down on the recliner, several feet away from the

lavender couch where he was relaxing, and bent down to cover my face with my hands.

"But we hate each other," I said, my voice sounding odd. "Why—"

"I don't hate you," he said abruptly.

"OK, maybe we don't hate each other anymore. Hate is a strong word. But we don't *like* each other, and we're not friends. We're certainly not *more than* friends. We're not … people who kiss!" I dared to look at him, and he looked relaxed but thoughtful. And then a thought occurred to me. "Well, it's Valentine's Day. Please tell me this isn't some weird sympathy thing because you overheard me talking to Mari about Valentine's Day and me being a romantic and—well, you felt sorry for me …" I trailed off.

His face transformed in an instant. Gone was the serious but almost oddly affectionate look from before. Now his expression was thunderous, and he sat up straighter, his body tense.

"Uh, did I say something?"

He looked at his hands, which were clenched, and then abruptly stood.

What on earth had ticked him off suddenly? Maybe my theory about the kiss being a pity kiss was wrong, but why would that trigger *this* strong of a reaction?

Without a word or even a glance, he darted over to the front door and stuffed his feet into his boots.

Perplexed, I rose and followed him. "Peter? Please, I'm so confused. What is going on?"

It all felt like a bad dream.

Well, except for the part that felt amazing. That part was glorious …

No, I was just tired, exhausted, caught off guard.

He turned toward me but avoided my eyes. "You're right. You don't need me here. Your heat seems to be working, and obviously your shower is too." I watched his Adam's apple bob as he swallowed.

I nodded, but my brows were furrowed. "Wait. Maybe we should talk—"

"I have to go," he said before turning around.

"Why now?" I cried in exasperation. "When I wanted you to leave me alone, you wouldn't … Peter, wait."

His hand still on the doorknob, he turned back to me, and his cool blue eyes met my eyes briefly. "Sorry, Hazel."

Before I could think of any response, he opened the door and stepped out, closing it behind him quickly.

I stepped back, shivering from the blast of frigid air from outside. But my skin quickly warmed as memories of our kiss came unbidden, all the little details flooding my mind, my senses.

I had to sit down.

"What just happened?"

Chapter 13

When the plow finally came through two days later, I hired a local guy to help clear my driveway and then drove into town for my monthly lunch with Nora, who was Terry's grandmother. We'd hit it off almost immediately just over a year ago when I was scheming with Mariana on how to convince Nora's wife, Jane, to sell the Christmas village. At the time, we didn't know Terry was Nora's grandson—he'd left out that little detail—and that trying to convince Jane to sell was futile since she and Nora had already planned to bequeath it to him. After Terry and Mariana reconciled a few weeks after Christmas, I called up Nora to ask if she wanted to meet me for coffee. The older lady was sweet and infinitely wise but also sassy and hilarious, just my kind of woman. That fifty-year age gap? Irrelevant.

While driving downtown, I debated on whether to talk to her about Peter and everything that had happened. Even after replaying Peter's visit in my head at least a dozen times over the next two days, I still had no idea what to think. As usual, the man was infuriating, but now he was confusing as well. I hadn't told Mariana anything yet because … well, it felt like a conflict of interest, with her being married to Peter's friend. She'd probably try to do some matchmaking or something. I'd talk to her eventually, but not yet.

As I pulled into the parking lot, I saw through the cafe window that Nora was waiting for me. Her thin, silver hair was barely visible beneath a cute yellow hat. In fact, I'd almost say the hat was what brought us together, as I never saw her without one. When I remarked on this, she'd said, "This beautiful brain needs to stay warm to be able to show its brilliance. Plus, there are just so many cute hats, right?" From then on, I knew we'd be great friends.

"Nora, so good to see you!" I exclaimed while removing my blue knit scarf and gloves.

She pulled me into a hug. "Hazel, you're more gorgeous than ever. It's been too long since we've met."

"Only a month," I squeaked as she crushed her surprisingly strong arms around me.

"But this past week has seemed like a year, am I right?"

"Tell me about it," I muttered as we stepped apart.

"Oh, I intend to," she said, her bright red lips curving into a smile.

I smiled back before realizing what this meant. She'd want to know what I'd done during the storm. There was no way to avoid this.

"From your face, I see a story," she said with a smirk.

I laughed, linking arms with her. "Let's go get a table first though."

After the server took our order, I complimented her. "I love your hat. Yellow suits you."

"It does, doesn't it?" She smiled while sipping from the water glass the server had brought out.

"So how are you, Nora? And how's Jane?"

"Well, I'm still alive," she said with twinkling eyes. Her standard reply.

"You're one of the healthiest, most energetic people I know, even at eighty-five. One day, I'll make you share your secrets."

"Good genes. In other words, luck," she said with a hint of something not quite happy. Hmm. That was new.

"And how is Jane?"

Her breath caught briefly, and she busied herself rearranging her napkin in her lap. "She's hanging in there." She paused, seemingly unsure whether she wanted to say more. "She won't admit to it, but I see her struggling."

My eyebrows drew together in sympathy. "Is it the sciatica again?"

"I think so. But she denies it when I ask and turns down offers of help. Never did I meet a more stubborn woman."

I couldn't help smiling. "Except maybe yourself."

Nora narrowed her eyes before returning the smile. "You have a point. I worry about her though, as she clammed up the last time I asked and didn't reschedule the last doctor's appointment. It was during the storm, so we had to cancel it, of course."

I nodded. "Understandable. Darn it, I wish I could help somehow. But she's as likely to listen to me as she is to grow wings."

We both laughed as the server came over with our spinach and artichoke dip appetizer.

After dipping the crusted bread and taking a first bite, Nora asked, "So, what's new with you? How's the writing going?"

I'd told her about my new career plans during our last lunch date, and she'd been supportive. "I hate to let you down, but it's not going the greatest. Writing is hard."

She tilted her head. "But you wrote a book before."

"Years ago, yes. But it was different. The words practically poured out of me, and the only problem was finding time to write, since I was always traveling on the speaking tours." I took a sip of water. "This time is different. I have a lot of time, so that's not the problem. Maybe it's writer's block, I don't know. I haven't gotten very far in my first draft, and I didn't get to meet with my agent because of the stupid storm. I was hoping she'd help me with the block. Anyway, it's slow going."

"I thought you liked writing?"

"I do, sometimes. But I don't want to *just* write. I feel like it's not fulfilling enough in itself. Being holed up at home in front of a computer isn't really me ... sometimes, sure, but not all the time. You know?"

Nora peered at me closely and nodded. "So, take your time on the book."

I considered this for a moment. "But—"

"Are you hurting for money? Is that it?" She stuck her bread in the dip.

"No. At least, not now. I have some savings, but it'll run out within a couple of years."

"You can do a lot in a couple years. Like I said, take your time." She shrugged and then dabbed at her mouth with her napkin.

"I guess there's no rush. My literary agent didn't give me a hard deadline, at least not yet. We're meeting next week. And I told Roxy I'm taking a break from speaking events." I paused, looking out the window. "But with all this downtime, I should be figuring things out. Deciding what I really want to be doing. Making plans, starting projects or maybe a new business—"

"Being busy, you mean? You're not busy and stressed all the time, so something feels off," Nora said with the confidence of a lifetime. "I went through that too."

"You did?"

"Yes, when I officially retired. And then *again* a year ago when Terry and Mari took over the Christmas village, including its finances." One side of her mouth curved upward. "You've got to figure out what you want to do, yes. But it doesn't have to be today. Or tomorrow or even this month."

I nodded slowly. "I guess so."

"And when you've got some ideas you want to bounce off someone who'll always tell it like it is, you know where to find me," she said with a smile.

I returned the smile just as our server returned with our food.

Nora had the same lunch she always ordered: an Italian sandwich with extra oil and vinegar. I liked to mix it up though rather than committing to just one dish.

"What is that?" she asked, pointing to my plate.

"Cajun shrimp with tomatoes and seasoned rice." I smiled

as the tempting smell filled my nostrils. "Didn't you hear me order it? It's a new menu item."

She made a face and bit into her sandwich. "So how about this weather we've had? It's one of the worst blizzards I've seen."

My eyes were wide. "Only *one* of the worst?"

"Hazel, dear, I've seen a lot of harsh winters and sweltering summers. This wasn't nearly as bad as the one in the '70s. That was before I met Janie."

"Wow. Well, I guess I'm glad I wasn't alive in that decade. This one was bad enough." I took my first bite of shrimp. "Ah, perfection. New Orleans was always one of my favorite places to travel."

"Janie and I went there once, even partied on Bourbon Street with a rock star. Meh, it was overrated."

My eyebrows rose as I chewed. "I don't even know where to begin responding to that statement."

She shrugged. "Then don't."

I suppressed a smile. "How did you and Jane hold up during the storm?"

"We were fine. With the wood stove, we stayed toasty warm."

"But no electricity—that was hard."

"I was born before electricity was invented, dear."

"Oh, right."

I was relieved that she and Jane had been fine. Perhaps it had even been cozy and romantic. I envied them.

"I'm joking, my dear. Electricity was invented in the nineteenth century. Most places had it when I was growing up. At least in Chicago where we were."

I smacked my forehead against my palm. "Of course. I knew that."

"You seem a little distracted." She studied me with interest.

My eyes shifted away for just a second. "Nope."

I wasn't still thinking about the jerk next door. The one who definitely hadn't felt like a jerk when we—

"If you say so." She scrunched her eyebrows together in doubt but then shrugged. "So, what did you do during the storm? Not much within walking distance where your house is."

I put my fork down. This was it. "My next-door neighbor had a generator, so I stayed at their house for a few days."

Her eyebrows rose slightly. "Oh, I didn't know you had a new neighbor. You never said."

"He just moved in a few weeks ago."

Now her eyebrows were halfway up her forehead. "*He*? I thought you said *they*."

"Oh, huh," I said casually. "Well, yes, *he* moved in a few weeks ago. He has a cat, so it's technically *they*."

She took a bite of the sandwich and eyed me as she chewed slowly.

"It's not a big deal. It was nice to have a place to shelter, that's all."

Nora smirked. "You're not a good liar."

I winced. "Dammit."

"Out with it, then."

"OK, yes, I have a new neighbor, but he's rude and condescending, and we don't like each other. But he let me stay, so I'm grateful for that."

A knowing smile graced her face. "Is he handsome?"

I laughed. "Like that matters. His generator worked great, and he helped me out. End of story."

"He's a looker then," she said before taking a sip of water.

Sighing, I stuffed a forkful of shrimp and rice into my mouth. "We don't get along though, Nora. We have nothing in common. He doesn't like me any more than I like him." I mean, none of it was fully true. We'd gotten along more than I expected. I wasn't about to admit that aloud though.

She nodded. "And yet you're attracted to him."

My mouth fell open. "I didn't say—"

"You didn't have to, dear."

"But I'm not—"

She rolled her eyes.

"Fine," I grumbled. "He's attractive, yes. And we had a little … moment. But we *really* don't like each other, so nothing further is going to happen." I looked at Nora's face, and surprisingly, she looked a bit sad. "What's wrong?"

She shook her head, as if she didn't realize she was showing any emotion. "Just want you to be happy, Hazel. I know you said a while back you're taking a break from dating." She waited until I nodded. "Maybe that's for the best. But maybe … I mean, all I'm saying is that we shouldn't let good opportunities pass us by."

I laughed with a touch of bitterness. "Trust me, he's not a good opportunity. He's not any kind of opportunity. He's moody, arrogant, rude … he's *complicated*. I don't need complicated. At least not now. I have enough to figure out with my career and, well, what I want to do with the rest of my life."

"You can just forget about that last thing. 'The rest of your life' doesn't exist. You only have the present. Sure, you can plan for the future, but don't feel like you have to figure everything out. You never will. And I should know." She smiled at me, and her small hand with purple nail polish covered mine. "Trust me."

I nodded. "That makes sense. Maybe I could take some pressure off."

"For Pete's sake, yes."

I must have made a face because she gave me a questioning look.

"Sorry, it's just … you said 'Pete.' And this guy's name is Peter."

Nora looked amused. "I knew a 'Pete' once. Sold furniture and was the most gregarious guy you'd ever meet. We used to play cards together … so much fun. Gosh, that was decades ago."

"That's lovely. But it sounds like the opposite of the Peter I know," I said dryly. "Especially the gregarious part."

Nora took the last bite of her sandwich, and when finished, she set her napkin on the table and looked at me thoughtfully. "If your Pete is complicated and you don't want complicated right now, then I think you have your answer."

I smiled in relief. Yes, that's what I wanted to hear. "Exactly. But he's not *my* Peter."

"Well, that remains to be seen," she said with a twinkle in her eye as I shook my head. That's another thing we had in common: she too was a hopeless romantic despite being a cynic in so many things. But the difference was she'd found the love of her life, whereas I … well, I wasn't sure if I ever would.

Chapter 14

I grinned at my best friend, whose blush always gave her away. "Fine, I'll give you a pass on sharing the juiciest details but only because you guys are so cute."

The color in Mariana's cheeks deepened. "Thanks, I think." She grinned back at me. "But enough about me. I want to hear about how you've been, Haz."

My smile faltered but only slightly. "I've been fine. I'm just so happy for you, Mari. After all this time, you deserve happiness. Cherish it."

"I'll make sure she does," said a male voice just before Terry appeared from the hallway.

"Hey, Pinecone, how are you?"

"Tired but happy," he said with a grin and tired eyes echoing his statement.

"Still jet-lagged?"

He yawned. "Yes, and my allergies are acting up."

Mariana rolled her eyes. "Men are such babies about sleep and sniffling."

I nodded. "True."

"But women love to complain about men every chance they get," he said with a smirk.

"Also true." I laughed and then watched as they smacked lips together.

I averted my eyes, feeling uncomfortable for some reason even though I'd seen them kiss a million times. Terry was all about the PDA, and even Mari had warmed up to it. It usually didn't bother me, but for some reason, it hit hard today that I was really superfluous here. Mari didn't need me anymore—not like she did before—and I was basically a third wheel.

"Get a room, newlyweds. You're so sickeningly sweet," I said, attempting a playful tone.

"Sorry," Mari said, swiping at her mouth after pulling away from him.

"I'm only kidding. Mostly."

She looked at me with concern, and a seed of discomfort grew within my stomach. "Hazel, are you OK? You seem ... I don't know. Something is off." She looked at Terry, squeezing his hand before letting it go. "Go back to watching the game. Girl talk is coming."

He put his hands up and laughed. "You don't need to ask me twice."

When he'd left the room, I took a deep breath for courage. "Mari, I do want to talk to you about ... how I've been doing."

Her expression was patient as she crossed her legs on the sofa. "Sure. We probably have at least twenty minutes before dinner is delivered."

"I believe I mentioned this when you called, but writing progress is slow. Beyond slow. I was hoping to write the book within six months, but at this rate, it'll be six years. Maybe more."

Her face was sympathetic, but her tone was firm. "You can't rush greatness. Seriously, take your time. I mean, yeah, if certain things are blocking you from writing, address those. You know I'll do my best to help. But writing a book takes time, I think. And you're going through a major career and life transition at the same time—it's only natural this wouldn't be easy."

I nodded slowly. "I suppose you're right. Nora said something similar."

She bit her lip and shifted her position as worry showed on her face. Finally, she spoke slowly, "I'm more worried about how you're coping with the bigger change, you know, staying home and not traveling and meeting people all the time." She paused. "I could see it on your face and hear it in your voice the last few times we talked."

"Yeah, I think you diagnosed me with cabin fever, and you'd be right," I said, trying to laugh it off. "I'll be OK though. I was actually really productive the past couple days and … well, just getting out of the house was nice, especially after the—" I stopped, not wanting to mention being snowed in with Peter and opening that can of worms. "Yeah, it was nice."

She smiled. "What did you do today?"

"First thing this morning, I called a service tech about fixing or replacing my crappy insulation, and then I went to the store to stock up on flashlights and lanterns. You know, for future preparedness. What else … I worked out at the gym instead of at home, and I stocked up on groceries. I even went to the library to write for a while."

"That's awesome! Some people prefer doing solitary work away from home. So it's solitary but not alone if that makes sense."

"I know. That might be my thing, but it's hard to say because I didn't write for very long today."

"It's new. You'll get used to it."

I hoped she was right. The knowledge that Peter was right next door didn't help though. But at least now I'd decided to stop hiding out in my house. If I saw him again—no, *when* I saw him again, because it was inevitable as neighbors—I'd play it cool. Be polite, courteous, and unaffected. So far, I hadn't seen him, but I also hadn't been sitting at my window-facing desk lately. Instead, I'd worked from the couch, the kitchen, or the library. Anywhere but the front window.

"Hazel, what else is going on?"

My eyes, which had been staring unseeing at the front window curtains, darted to hers. "Nothing."

Her eyes narrowed. "Really? With you, nothing always means something."

"Why does that statement sound so familiar?" I smiled

wryly. "Oh, maybe because I've said it to *you* so many times."

"Fair enough. But you're deflecting." She peered at me closely before adding, "Tell me about the storm. I can't believe Peter lives next to you and let you stay at his house!"

"Yeah, it's bizarre. For a moment, I thought maybe you and Terry somehow engineered it." Actually, I still wondered about that. I watched her closely for her reaction.

She gasped. "Hazel, we would never ... OK, well, maybe we would. I wish we had thought of it. But alas, we didn't." She flashed a sheepish smile.

I laughed. "At least you're honest."

She flushed. "Well, about that—"

The doorbell rang before she could finish her sentence. She turned shifty eyes toward the front door, and I listened as Terry descended the stairs.

"Where did you order food from?" I asked calmly. But I had a sinking feeling.

"Village Pizzeria," she mumbled as her eyes returned to me.

Dammit.

"Mari, do you have something to tell me?" I asked when we heard Terry saying hello around the corner.

She bit her lip. "I was just about to tell you."

I sighed deeply. "You didn't. Please tell me—"

"Ladies, our fourth is here!" Terry called out, walking into the room with a wide smile.

I squeezed my eyes shut tight, wishing I was anywhere but here. But when my eyes reluctantly opened, there he was.

The man I'd tried to stop thinking about these past few days. I had no reason to be thinking about him. It was infuriating. And why, oh why, did he look more handsome than ever tonight? He was clean-shaven, he'd had a haircut, and he was wearing chinos and a golf shirt. A preppy look that usually didn't do it for me. But on him, well, I had to force myself to not openly ogle him.

Leaning closer to Mari, I hissed, "You didn't think to warn

me?"

She winced. "Sorry. I only found out just before you came that Terry invited him, and I thought we'd have time to talk about it."

I pressed my lips together and nodded curtly to him. Our eyes met, and he said nothing.

"Hi, Peter! So glad you could make it. Welcome!" my best friend said to my nemesis.

"Thank you, Mariana," he said, dipping his head. "You have a lovely home."

She and Terry smiled at one another and then thanked Peter, while I sat with my arms crossed.

Maybe I could think of an excuse to cancel on dinner. I loathed lying though, and I missed Mari so much. Still, was it worth having to share space with Peter again, albeit only for a meal? I mean, he had *kissed* me. Passionately. And then abruptly stormed out. We hadn't talked or even seen each other since. This was taking awkward to a whole new level.

"Mari, do you want any wine, or are you still—"

"Still abstaining," I said reluctantly. I didn't intend to quit drinking forever, but I was hoping to get more than one and a half months without alcohol. I had to prove to myself that I could. But part of me longed for the liquid courage that I used to rely on around awkward date situations. Not that this was any kind of date. Definitely not. "I don't mind if anyone else drinks though."

After some small talk where I looked everywhere *but* at Peter, the pizza delivery finally came. We all shuffled into the dining room, where Mari had set up some fruit and veggie trays and candles.

Ugh, candles.

I peered at her closely as she sat at the head of the table. Had she envisioned this to be like a double date? I hoped not. I didn't want to disappoint her, but I would if I had to.

Wondering if Peter was having similar suspicions, I stole a glance at him as he pulled out the chair on the opposite side of the modest-sized table. As though he knew I was checking him out, his eyes zeroed in on me.

I quickly looked away, wondering if I had erred in declining a glass of wine.

So I focused on eating as Mari chatted with Peter, trying to draw him out a bit. Unsurprisingly, she was not successful, as he gave only short answers, albeit polite ones. His cool blue eyes flickered to mine more often than was necessary, even though I'd hardly spoken.

"You're quiet, Haz," Terry said after swallowing a mouth of meat pizza.

I slowly finished chewing my margherita slice and then took a sip of water, trying to stall as my mind frantically tried to figure out how to deflect the sudden attention. "Am I?" I asked breezily. "This pizza is just so good."

Peter spoke up—the first time he'd addressed me tonight— and his voice seemed deeper, richer than usual. "You appeared to be deep in thought."

I laughed. "Meditating on how delicious the food is, that's all."

Mari shook her head, probably seeing right through my pathetic answer. "Are you thinking about the book again?" Before I could answer, she turned to the men. "Hazel has been writing a book, and she's looking at a career move."

I nodded, eyeing my plate. I tried to think of some way to end this conversation before it went anywhere, but instead, I noticed a giant tomato stain on my white sleeve. Putting my arm under the table, I tried to discreetly rub it with my napkin, but it probably only made the stain worse.

When I looked up again, everyone was gazing at me with curiosity.

I rolled my eyes. "I spilled a little. Not a big deal. Mari, you were saying something about renovations in the village earlier, weren't you?"

"I was, yes. Starting with the library. Of course, we don't own the library, but we offered to organize a funding drive for the town." She looked at Terry and Peter then. "Hazel has started using the library for work. For writing her book, that is."

I clenched my teeth. She'd again placed the spotlight on me, where it wasn't welcome. I took a drink of water, now fully regretting my decision not to get intoxicated. "Yep."

But she and Terry *had* drunk some wine, and it was starting to show already. "Hazel, I've been thinking …" she said in that slow voice she always used when slightly tipsy, which was rare. "Have you ever thought that the full-time writer life isn't for you? I mean, maybe it is. But it doesn't have to be. There are *so* many other worthy things you could do to share your … your Hazel-ness with the world."

"My Hazel-ness," I repeated with a chuckle. But then I grimaced, realizing she was waiting for an answer. And we had an audience. "You're probably right."

"I have an idea!" Her eyes were bright as she looked briefly at Terry and then at me. "We could help you brainstorm some ideas!"

"Uh, sure. Maybe next time we have lunch—"

Terry held a hand up. "Why not right now? We're all together. Pizza is excellent brain food, after all."

"I'm not sure that's true—" I started.

"Wonderful idea!" my best friend beamed before blowing Terry a kiss.

I had to look away. "OK, I guess we're doing this." I sighed. "Well, I have considered opening a counseling service."

Her eyes lit up. "Hazel, what a wonderful idea! You'd be the best—oh, wait, don't you have to be certified for that?"

"Well, yes. I believe that's necessary to call yourself a counselor, so I thought about starting as a life coach, which doesn't require a degree. Then—"

"Then, if you like it, you could go get your degree?" I think this was the most excited I've ever seen her. She wasn't the bubbly sort at all, but the wine was obviously relaxing her. When I nodded, she added, "Oh, I just love this idea! Guys, isn't it wonderful?"

Terry's smile matched Mari's, but Peter merely nodded, his face revealing none of his feelings—if the man had any.

"What's wrong, Haz?"

I bit my lip when realizing I must have been frowning or, worse, staring at him. "Nothing. I … I'm glad you like my idea. I literally only thought about it this morning. I don't know for sure—I mean, there would be a lot of details to figure out."

"Roxy can help! She's amazing at coordinating all the details of things. And to be honest, she's seemed a bit … I don't know, restless the past six months or so. Maybe she's bored? This could be something new and interesting to work on."

The gears in my head were turning as I nodded slowly. "You know, that's a great idea. I'll call her tomorrow."

"Is she that quiet girl I met at the resort that one time— the one who didn't come to our wedding?" Terry asked, looking between Mari and me.

"That's her," Mari said. "She's really shy. But super sweet and amazing at what she does."

I nodded. "She's awesome. I just haven't spoken to her much since I haven't had any events for her to plan." I took a sip of water as they looked at me in expectation. "All right, I'll get in touch with her soon."

When I had casually mulled over this new idea this morning, one issue had lodged itself in my brain and refused to leave. I debated on bringing it up to Mari now, but I'd rather wait until we were alone.

"Spill, Haz. What's wrong?"

My eyes were wide as they landed on my friend. "How do you always know—"

"I've been studying up on emotional intelligence."

"Seriously?" I chuckled. "That's interesting."

"You didn't know her back then," Terry said, turning to Peter, "but my wife used to be the most anti-emotion person I'd ever met."

"Anti-emotion person?" Peter repeated, his lips twitching ever so slightly.

"You know what I mean, man," Terry said, elbowing his friend. "She was—"

"I'm here, you know," Mari said, scowling at Terry for a moment before she laughed. "It's OK, I don't mind admitting it. Anti-emotion definitely described how I used to be, before falling in love."

"Again," I chimed in. When she shot a questioning look my way, I added, "Falling in love again."

Her smile was brilliant as she nodded. "Yes. But stop distracting me. You were about to tell us something, Haz."

I shook my head even while smiling. "All right, it's just—most body image coaching programs and the like are prohibitively expensive. I have a lot of peers in this field who are amazing women, but their rates are only affordable for wealthy people. They do have some middle-class clients, but they tend to be short term, not enough time to truly resolve their issues, since it costs so much to continue longer term. And for lower-class people, there's virtually no access at all. A few get lucky with a good therapist covered by their insurance, but that's rare. I want—I want to be able to help people of all income levels. I'd love to reach people who'd never be able to afford this kind of help otherwise." I paused, smiling briefly. "But I also have to make a living. So, therein lies the problem."

The table went silent as everyone stared at me for a long moment.

Eventually, I saw tears welling up in Mariana's eyes. She placed her hand on her chest before speaking. "Hazel, this is— I love this so much. You know—you know I came from nothing. So I know better than anyone how being poor can be a blocker to treatment, especially mental health, but all kinds. Sometimes I wonder if my dad would've survived if ...." She trailed off, hiccupping through her tears. "Anyway, I love it."

Terry had reached across the table to hold her hand, looking a bit stunned since Mari never cried. He nodded at me. "It's a great idea, Hazel."

Peter cleared his throat, and my eyes reluctantly moved to

him. He was looking at his glass as he said, "You can apply for funding, from investors and sponsors."

My eyes widened. "That's … true. I don't know why I didn't think of that." The best idea of the night, coming from *him*? The world seemed upside down. "Thank you."

He merely nodded before taking a sip of his water. He'd also said no to the wine tonight, I noticed.

Finally, the conversation moved away from me and my life for the rest of the evening, until we were heading toward the front door to leave. We were talking about exercise as I pulled on my coat, and out of nowhere, Terry exclaimed, "Hey, I just had the best idea."

I turned to him warily, as he was more than a little tipsy.

"Peter here goes on walks every day, he just said." Terry pointed to Peter as if I didn't know who he was. As if I didn't know about the daily walks. Well, I couldn't blame him for not knowing that. "Hazel, you said you've been bored with working out at home, and Zumba classes are always crowded this time of year. But you guys live right next to each other—you could go walking together!"

My head whipped around as I shot Mariana a look of horror, a *you-must-stop-this* pleading look. But she was smiling and looking at Terry.

"Oh, I couldn't—I wouldn't want to impose. Surely Peter loves taking *solitary* walks. It can be so meditative, you know?"

The silence was especially awkward as I fumbled with a zipper that was stuck. Finally, as I pulled it loose, I heard his deep voice. "I do enjoy solitary walks. But I don't mind if Hazel joins me."

I shook my head vehemently. "No, it's fine. You have your walks, and I'll find—there are so many different things to do at the gym. I'll be fine."

Mari looked between us, and I couldn't decipher her expression. "But being out in nature is so much better for you. Don't you think, Peter?"

"I do."

"Well, that's settled then. You two can start walking together. It'll be a chance to get to know each other better." Her eyes were shining as she looked at each of us. "This was so fun. We *have* to do this again."

I groaned inwardly while attempting a smile. I didn't have the heart to say no, not when she looked *so happy*. This was not the Mari I'd known for so many years. I wanted to cry tears of joy when I saw the joy on her face. She was such a good person; she deserved to be happy.

But I also wanted to scream, because … what had she just signed me up for?

Chapter 15

I was finishing up a video call with Roxy the next day when the doorbell rang.

"Hang on, Roxy, I've got to answer the door," I said.

"It's OK. We're done anyway," she said. "Bye, Hazel."

"Bye—" And she'd already hung up. OK then. She was such a kind, thoughtful woman, but she was also ruthless about efficiency. I think she hated the idea of using someone's time, which usually stemmed from low self-esteem, feeling unworthy of someone's time. I smiled while walking to the front door. I was already starting to think like a real counselor, and I hadn't even started yet!

After pulling open the front door though, I felt my smile slip.

"Hello," Peter said. "Ready to walk?" He looked down at my long-sleeve T-shirt and shorts and frowned.

"Oh. Um … really?" I gripped the edge of the door.

"Yes, I walk at this time every day."

"I know, but—" Oh no, did I just admit to knowing his routine? I felt my face flush. "We don't have to do this, you know."

"Don't you want to walk?"

"No? I mean, I don't *not* want to walk, but I meant—" I paused, taking a long breath. "It just felt like Mari decided this for us, so I'm just saying that we don't need to."

"If you don't want to go, that's fine," he said, his face stoic.

"I—it's not that I don't want to."

"Then you do want to?"

I let out an exasperated sigh. "I don't know. I hadn't thought about it. And I'm not dressed for it."

"I'll wait."

I opened my mouth to speak but then closed it. Shrugging, I turned around and went to my bedroom to change.

It might be better to just get this over with.

We'll both see how awkward it is, and he won't ask me again.

Problem solved.

At least in theory.

But as we walked a long loop in what was a cool but surprisingly invigorating February day, I wasn't hating it. In fact, I felt a tiny bit sad when we rounded the corner and our houses came into view. We'd barely spoken. But it was—well, if I didn't know how much we disliked each other, I'd almost call it a companionable silence.

When we reached his house, I expected we'd say goodbye, but he kept walking with me all the way to my door.

"Um, thanks," I said, turning around once I reached the porch and he stood below the steps. "I guess … have a nice day."

He nodded, and maybe he would have replied, but I flashed a polite smile and turned quickly to go into my house. I shut the door without looking back at him and slumped against it.

It was a surprisingly good walk.

So what was this angst in the pit of my stomach?

As I took off my coat and boots, I vowed to not think about it. It was a pleasant excursion, but probably a one-time thing. Surely he'd see that we weren't compatible as friends—if he didn't already see that—and he wouldn't ask me to accompany him again.

*****

Two days later, I was exhausted from staying up almost all night. The previous afternoon I'd met with Roxy along with Jeff, who was Mariana's financial advisor. Feeling inspired, I'd spent the entire evening hunched over my computer jotting down ideas and research for my new business idea. Needless to say, I was exhausted this morning when Sofia called me at 9 am, as I'd only gone to bed two hours earlier.

Supportive as ever, Sofia had many tips to share on overcoming writer's block while also giving me some firm nudges to get to work. I decided to commit to doing a small amount of writing and/or book research each day—a modest amount, really, but it would help me to avoid overwhelm.

Still, trying to write on only two hours of sleep wasn't working well, and I was struggling to focus on the screen as I lay half-reclined on the couch with my laptop.

I could take a nap.

Naps always helped.

Somehow, I managed to drag myself off the couch to nap in my bedroom, where my night cap and cozy blankets were. I'd just taken off my slippers when I heard knocking.

With my brows furrowed, I wondered who that could be. Everyone I knew always used the doorbell. Yawning, I padded to the front door in my bare feet and opened the door.

The cool blue eyes captured my attention first, followed by the rosy cheeks and visible exhalation from the mouth of one Peter Auclair. The mouth I'd kissed.

Why did I think of *that*?

I was sure my cheeks were rosy too as I swallowed and greeted him.

"Hello, Hazel," he said with his usual fixed expression. "Are you ready?"

I squinted at his face and then looked around us both as if there was something or someone else I'd missed. "What—ready for what?"

Impatience briefly flared on his face before he said, "For our walk."

My mind raced as I fumbled through words. "For—uh, did we—I'm sorry. I don't think I remember making plans with you today." Or ever.

I was exhausted, but I'm pretty sure I would've remembered agreeing to another walk.

He sighed. "You agreed to accompany me on my daily walks. Did you forget what time?"

My mouth gaping, I nodded and then shook my head.

"You must have forgotten. That's why you didn't answer the door yesterday."

He came over yesterday?

What?

"Um, I had a business meeting yesterday afternoon. Sorry you came when I wasn't here. But—"

"It's fine. Can you hurry and get ready? It's cold just standing here." I noticed a muscle ticked in his jaw.

I took a steadying breath. "I didn't think—we weren't really—" I looked into his eyes then, which held a hint of vulnerability. I probably imagined it, but I paused to consider my next words. "Do you really want to start walking together every day?" I could hear the disbelief in my voice.

He sighed. "Yes." His eyes never left mine. "That's why I'm here. We agreed, did we not?"

"Well ... OK, sure."

What harm would it do? I sensed I'd be somehow hurting his feelings if I said no, it was all a misunderstanding. But that was kind of ridiculous because he wasn't the type to have hurt feelings over something so trivial. Right? Though I didn't really know him that well, did I?

Our eyes were still locked, but I offered a small smile and told him I'd be right back. I wasn't dressed for a cold winter day, though I did notice the sun was shining at least.

A few minutes later, we were setting off in the same direction he always took, past the old, abandoned farm and around a long loop. We were both quiet, which was fine by me.

"You seem very tired," he remarked after we'd walked a quarter of a mile.

"Oh, do I? Sorry," I said, flashing an apologetic smile.

"You've yawned eight times in four minutes."

My eyes widened as I stole a glance at him. "Wow, you're very observant."

He said nothing to this.

"Sorry, it's rude. I was actually about to take a nap when you arrived. I didn't really sleep last night."

He was silent for a long moment, so I figured he wouldn't reply. Why would he? It's not like he cared about my sleep.

But he surprised me. "Out late last night?"

I looked over at him, but he was looking straight ahead. "Uh, no. Just working late. You know, the new business idea we talked about at Mari's house."

He glanced over at me then. "I'm relieved."

What? Why would he be relieved?

He was relieved that I wasn't out late? I mean, why would he care—

"I'm relieved that the new business idea seems promising and you're making progress. But you need to take care of yourself," he said, his tone more authoritative than I'd like.

I gave him a side-eye but said nothing. It was none of his business. It's not like we were even friends.

Why were we even walking together? He seemed like the sort of person who'd enjoy solitary walks—prefer them, even. I'd given him plenty of outs.

"So, have you always walked at the same time every afternoon?" I asked, keeping my tone light.

"No." I thought he wasn't going to say anymore, but finally, he continued, "As CEO, I never had time. Or interest. I usually went to the gym before work to lift weights and run on the treadmill. Higher intensity meant more efficient use of time."

"We have a couple of gyms here in Shipsvold if you're into that," I offered. I wasn't going to tell him which gym I belonged to though. The last thing I needed when getting my sweat on was to be distracted by him in his gym shorts or—

What the heck? End this line of thought now.

He sighed deeply. "No, thank you."

I waited for him to say more, but when he didn't, I probed, "You decided you prefer walking over the gym now?"

"It's not about what I like or dislike. Exercise is for health." He sighed again. "The cardiologist said low- to moderate-intensity exercise would be better, at least for the time being as we monitor my health condition. He suggested outdoor walks."

"Ah." That made a lot more sense. He wasn't the type of man who enjoyed taking long walks in nature, and this time of year was so cold and miserable. "Is there a reason you walk at the exact same time every day?"

As soon as the words were spoken, I wanted to disappear. Now it would be obvious I'd paid more than a little attention to his walking habits. I looked away, trying to think of a way to change the subject immediately.

But it didn't seem to faze him. "I like my days to have structure. It's one of the most difficult things about this … transition. I'm used to having a regimented schedule dictated by critical tasks, responsibilities, and obligations to others."

I nodded though he wasn't looking at me. "That's very obvious about you. So I imagine this, well, this life change hasn't been easy for you."

He shrugged. "It's fine."

But I could tell it was anything but fine. It struck me then that he felt lost, just like I did. Coping with a change in life goals, activities, environs—a complete life change—was hard. And perhaps doubly so for Peter, since he hadn't really had a choice in the matter. I felt a pang of something in my chest, a tether to him that … well, I didn't know how to feel about that.

We walked in silence for a few minutes before I asked gently, "Have you figured out what you're going to do now? In terms of work? Or are you just retiring early?"

When I looked at him, his face showed a flicker of discomfort, but it was so brief I might've imagined it. "I have a couple of ideas, but it's uncertain."

"Well, shoot."

He looked at me then, his expression neutral. "Excuse me?"

"Hit me with your ideas." When his brow furrowed, I added, "I was coerced into sharing my big idea the other night at dinner, before it was even close to ready for public consumption. Your turn." I laughed to try to set him at ease.

It didn't work though, as he sighed yet again, twice, before finally responding, "I thought about inquiring about part-time positions in data analysis or finance. Ideally both. I'd run it by the doctors though."

"Sounds scintillating."

He glanced at me then, and I didn't look away. "It can be."

"I'm teasing. I can appreciate that. I used to kind of enjoy reading law briefs, sometimes. I made the mistake of saying that out loud at a party one time, and let's just say I cleared the room."

He glanced at me with what I might've identified as a smile if it hadn't been so quick. We walked in silence for a minute as we trudged through a snowy section that clearly hadn't been plowed yet.

"I've inquired about volunteer positions at the shelter. I meet with the director on Friday."

My eyes widened. "A homeless shelter?"

"Animal shelter," he replied.

My jaw dropped. "Seriously?"

I couldn't picture him working with animals. At all.

Was he joking? Then again, I'd never heard him joke about anything.

He gave me a quizzical look. "Yes, why wouldn't I be serious?"

"It's just … I wouldn't have pegged you as an animal person. I mean, you have a cat, but …" I waved a hand vaguely, unsure what else to say without offending him.

After a pause, he replied, "You make a lot of assumptions about me."

I scoffed, "What? No, I don't."

He said nothing but glanced over at me briefly.

In the silence, I pondered what he'd said. Had I assumed a lot about him? In my view, I just made some reasonable deductions based on what I'd seen from him. I wasn't the type to judge prematurely.

Was I?

I frowned, realizing I wasn't the most objective person in this scenario. Maybe I'd ask Mari. She'd be honest.

An idea popped in, and I looked at him, seeing no visible emotion. "Hey, feel free to say no, but would you like to carpool on Friday? You said you're going into town, and I was planning to drop my car off to change the tires, so I need a ride home. The shelter isn't far from the auto shop. I mean, technically, nothing in Shipsvold is very far from anything. Because, you know, small town."

I was rambling again. I peered at him to see if he looked annoyed, but his face looked thoughtful. After a moment, he nodded. "Yes, that's fine."

We walked along in silence for a few minutes, and I almost fell on my face in a particularly icy patch as we rounded the curve back toward our houses. I clumsily grabbed onto his jacket to catch my balance, and he held my elbow as a righted myself.

I tried not to jerk my arm back once I was completely vertical again.

"So, how's Randy doing?"

"He's good."

"Does he miss me?" I laughed and then I wondered why I asked that. "Just kidding."

"I think he does, actually," Peter said, glancing at me before stepping around another icy patch. "He seems bored with me. But I've applied to adopt another cat from the shelter, so he may have a playmate soon."

I was still struggling to reconcile that he was not only a cat person but also someone who wanted to work with rescue animals—even adopting them. It didn't fit at all with my vision of him. "So, are you one of those people who like animals more than people?" I blurted out.

He was silent for a long moment, and I wondered if he was offended. "I like a few people. But yes, in general, I prefer animals." He paused. "We had a cat and a dog growing up, and they were my best friends."

My eyes widened. This *really* didn't fit my vision of him. Did I even know him at all? I couldn't imagine him as this child whose best friends were his pets. Then again, I couldn't really imagine him as a child at all.

The sound he made almost seemed like a laugh, but he cleared his throat instead. "I was a child once, yes."

Oh, crap, had I said that aloud?

"Sorry, sometimes my filter malfunctions."

He made another raspy noise that sounded suspiciously like a chuckle. "It's fine. I prefer honesty and directness anyway."

I was going to scream if I heard him say *It's fine* one more time. I didn't want fine. I wanted … well, I didn't know.

"Well, here we are," he said as we reached a spot about halfway between our houses. I tried but failed to cover another yawn. "You look tired. Please rest."

"Yes, sir." I saluted him.

Because apparently I said and did weird things around this guy.

His eyes held mine for a few more seconds before his lips curved upward slightly and he turned to leave.

Apparently my stomach did weird things too.

Chapter 16

"**A**rgh. I forgot to collect my money after passing Go! I'll just take it now—"

"Nope. Against the rules. You have to collect it during your turn."

My jaw dropped. "Whose rules? I don't remember reading that." I giggled. "Then again, has anyone ever read the Monopoly rules? Everyone I know puts money in the middle and collects it when they land on Free Parking, yet the rules say nothing happens on that space."

"House rules. I can't allow you to break them."

I nearly fell off my chair then because his face suddenly transformed.

His lips were curved upward in a full-on smile with *dimples,* and it was an assault on my senses. On my mental capacity.

I must have looked as woozy as I felt because his smile dropped, replaced by a frown. "Are you all right?" He sighed. "Fine, we can make an exception to the rule this once."

I shook my head. "No, I … yes, I'm OK. And yes, give me my damn two hundred dollars." I pasted a smile on my face to hide the feeling building in me …

I was freaking out.

Who was this man who suddenly smiled—who let me break a rule? We'd been walking together daily for a few weeks now, and the change was so gradual I didn't notice until now.

He was different. More thoughtful. Even a little playful at

times.

I think we were actually friends now.

Friends!

I *never* would've imagined sitting here playing a board game on a Friday night with my grumpy neighbor. By choice. Not because of a natural disaster or an electrical problem. Just because we wanted to.

I wasn't even sure whose idea it had been. During a walk last week, we'd been talking about the board game, and then I ended up coming over to play it after dinner that night. And again a few nights later. And again.

I absently reached into our shared bowl of popcorn—low-salt and low-butter to make his doctor happy—and felt a jolt of electricity when my hand brushed his. I tried not to jerk my hand back because, well, I didn't want him to think I hated him anymore.

Because I didn't.

Not even close.

We were friends.

And I couldn't stop staring at his hand I'd just touched so lightly. And his face that had lost some of its severity and rigidness over the past weeks. His biceps that had flexed when he'd worn a short-sleeve shirt last night during our game. And those ocean blue eyes ...

Get it together, Hazel. He sees only you as a friend.

And that was fine.

Completely *fine*.

But that pang I felt in my chest ... that wasn't fine.

Even if there was some chance of becoming more than friends, it would be so complicated. My feelings, his, our status as neighbors, our best friends being married to each other ... all of it added up to *complicated*, and I didn't want complicated.

When his brow furrowed, I gave him a shaky smile to reassure him I was fine. Just fine. His favorite word. "It's your turn, Mr. Rulemaker."

His lips quivered again, and I swore he was about to smile

again, but thankfully I was saved from having to fight through all the feelings *that* event would've aroused again. The doorbell had rung.

I looked at him in confusion. Who on earth could it be? From what I could tell, he rarely had visitors. Really only Terry, from what I'd seen. And I knew Terry was in St. Paul with Mari tonight—something about a possible buyer for the Christmas tree farm, but I hadn't listened closely.

"I'll get rid of them. Be right back," he said, rising quickly.

Once he opened the door, a woman spoke with what sounded like an excited tone, though I couldn't make out her words. My stomach churned as I wondered why a woman would show up unexpectedly on a weeknight. Or any night. It shouldn't matter, I knew.

A minute or so later, he appeared in the doorway to the sitting room where I was still sitting in front of the fireplace with the game board.

His face was red, and he looked more uncomfortable than I'd ever seen him. "Hazel, I have a guest." Even his voice sounded strange.

A tall, striking middle-aged woman walked in then, with blonde hair that looked a little too perfect and azure eyes that I assumed were colored contact lenses. Her eyebrows rose in surprise as she took me in and then looked back to Peter. "You have a guest, love. Care to introduce us?"

I scrambled to my feet, hastily wiping a popcorn kernel off my lap as I forced a smile.

Peter sighed and pinched the bridge of his nose. "Mother, this is Hazel. Hazel, apparently my mother has decided to visit without any notice."

His mother's smile faded as she looked from me to him. "I did try to reach you a few weeks ago. I'm fairly sure I left a voicemail. Don't you remember?"

He looked at his mother with suspicion in his eyes. "I recall you promising you'd visit me in Chicago *last year*."

She blinked rapidly, and her lips quivered before she said

softly, "Oh, you know how it is. Randall can't get away very often because Jared needs him on the campaign. Of course, Randall's only helping with strategy at this point, not going out on the campaign trail." She beamed and then turned to me. "Randall is my husband, a retired Senator, and Jared is our son, who holds his Senate seat now."

My gaze swung to Peter, who was barely containing his anger. "Oh, so Jared is your brother? I didn't know you had any siblings."

"Stepbrother," he said, crossing his arms over his chest with a severe frown. "He's the son of my mother's second husband."

She waved her hand dismissively. "We're all family, that's what matters." She smiled at me.

"Ah," I said softly. I hadn't even known his parents were divorced. I knew next to nothing about his life before and outside of Shipsvold, for that matter. "Well, it's nice to meet you …"

"Call me Glenda," she said with another warm smile. "It is lovely to meet you too."

"Hazel and I were in the middle of something, as you can see," he said, his voice containing a warning note. "Did you plan on staying the night—"

She laughed. "Oh, no. I have a hotel room booked. Don't worry about that. Though I see your new home is lovely. Stately. Even Randall would be impressed."

Peter looked as though he couldn't care less what Randall thought, but he refrained from commenting. "So, what are you doing here?"

Her smile dropped briefly before she recovered. "I'm here to see my son, of course. Can we sit down?" She looked over at me. "I'm truly sorry to interrupt. It's not often I get to see my son though."

"It's not often you *choose* to see your son," he snapped. After a long inhale and exhale, he said, "Fine, let's sit down."

"I should go," I said, stepping back around the other side of the couch as if to fade into the background. "I was—"

"No, Hazel," he barked. When my eyes widened, he added more softly, "Stay. Please."

Part of me wanted to leave this weird, painfully awkward encounter as soon as possible. Another part of me perceived his words as a plea for moral support—not that he'd *ever* phrase it that way. He didn't want to be alone with her, for some reason. He needed me. Plus, I was curious, so I shrugged and followed them to sit on one of the couches.

His mother watched our interaction with decided interest but merely smiled brightly at me and said nothing. I didn't know whether to trust her smile—it looked genuine, but she was a politician's wife, after all.

"So how are you doing, darling? I had to hear it from your father that you have health issues. Stress-induced heart issues, he said ... well, I guess you get that from him. But are you healthy? That's far more important than keeping your father's company alive." She pursed her lips. "I don't like having to hear this kind of news from that man." *That man* being her ex-husband, I assumed. The pinched look on her face confirmed it.

The muscles in Peter's jaw flexed, and I could see how much effort he put into responding in an even tone. "I'm better. And I didn't want to bother you. I know how busy you are."

"Never too busy for my oldest son, darling."

He scoffed. "Right. I haven't heard from you since Christmas. And I am your *only* son, Mother."

"Well, you know Jared is like a son to me." She turned to me. "He was only four years old when I married Randall. His mother sadly passed a few years ago, so I'm the only mother figure in his life now."

"Considering that he's a grown man, I'm not sure he needs a mother figure in his life."

I could tell *that* stung. Her hands shook a bit as she shifted in her seat. Still, she raised her chin. "Everyone needs a mother."

"You could've fooled me," he muttered.

I didn't *think* the woman was going to cry, but I didn't

want to take any chances, so I decided to interject. "Peter, why don't you tell her about—"

He shook his head rapidly, so I stopped. I looked over helplessly at Glenda, but she was fumbling around in her purse. She pulled out her phone and started scrolling before looking up briefly at us. "Just a moment ..."

"By all means, take your time," he said dryly.

"Aha, here it is!" She held the phone out to him. "Look at my call log, darling. I *did* try to reach you. It was on February 14 at 9:30 ..." The words died on her lips as she glanced up at Peter and then lowered the phone to her lap. "Peter, darling, are you OK?"

His face was red and his breathing erratic as he stared at her and then clenched his fists tight as he rose and bolted out of the room.

Shocked, I gasped and looked at Glenda. "Oh my—do you think he's OK? Maybe one of us should go after him?"

Glenda's face was white as she shakily placed her phone back in her purse and stood. "No, I—I should go. It's late, and I still need to drive to the hotel. You ... you can check on him, right?"

I stared at her, confusion and shock swirling through me. She looked so shaken, but ... she was just going to *leave*?

And more importantly, what was going on with him?

I rose to my feet as well. "All right, if you need to go ... well, I'll tell him you left."

"Thank you, dear. I ... I will—please tell him I'll be in touch." And then she hurried to the front entrance and donned her coat before leaving.

What kind of mother just *leaves*—

I shook my head. There was no time to speculate.

I needed to find him.

*****

Sitting in the waiting room was one of the hardest things I'd done in a *long* time. My adrenaline started to wane, and I was alone except for a young couple huddled together and nearly asleep on the other side of the room.

I'd found Peter in his bedroom breathing rapidly and confused about his surroundings, and his pulse was off the charts. Panicked, I'd called 911, and we'd ridden together in an ambulance to the small hospital in a neighboring town. I wasn't allowed to accompany him further than check-in, and when the receptionist assured me we'd fly him to St. Paul if needed, fear gripped me.

Was this a heart attack? Something similar or even worse? I had no experience dealing with heart-related symptoms, as we had no heart issues in my family—though we had breast cancer and leukemia, which were arguably just as bad if not worse.

I tried asking questions to the receptionist, but she knew nothing. When a doctor with a tablet in his hand finally came into the waiting room what felt like hours later, I jumped to my feet, but he turned to the young couple instead. I plopped down, defeated. Taking out my phone, I checked my texts again. I'd texted both Mari and Terry, and they hadn't responded yet. I'd also texted Nora and a few local friends, but I wasn't going to ask them to come wait with me—after all, they didn't even know Peter. He wouldn't like to have unfamiliar visitors, probably.

I clutched my stomach as it cramped, my fear worsening the longer I sat in wait. Would the doctors come find me if things were dire? I hoped so, but … I couldn't think about that. It couldn't be dire.

He had to be OK.

I needed him to be OK.

I tried some slow breaths to calm down, but the results were limited. During my fourth set of counting breaths, a nurse appeared in the room.

"You're here for Peter Auclair? You can see him now. Come with me." She looked tired and wasn't smiling, but her voice was friendly enough.

I practically ran over to her. "Is he OK? Is he going to die?

Please—"

She eyed me with sympathy. "He's not going to die. Don't worry."

Relief coursed through me until I remembered death was not the only dire outcome here. "Is he—"

"He's in this room," she interrupted as she stopped and pointed.

I bit my lip. "Can I … is it OK to talk to him? Or should I stay quiet?"

The nurse chuckled. "Oh, you can talk to him all you want. I don't know if he'll talk back though." At my expression of terror, she added, "Oh, I didn't mean it like that. He's fully capable of speech. I think he's just the quiet type. You know, reserved." Then she mumbled, "And stubborn."

Relief started to seep in as I managed a small smile. "Yes, he is. Thank you so much!"

I didn't hear what she said as I darted into the room. When I closed the door with a click, his gaze swung from the window to me.

He looked tired, a bit dazed, as he reclined on the hospital bed that looked tiny relative to his substantial height.

"Peter." My voice was barely above a whisper, as I didn't want to alarm him. "How are you feeling?"

"I'm fine now," he said. "Sorry you had to witness that." I watched as he tried to sit up but then decided against it.

"Don't apologize, Peter. I was so worried—but never mind that. You're going to be OK, and that's what matters."

He nodded once. "Yeah."

"I've never seen you look so relaxed," I said with a small smile.

He took a moment to respond. "It's the drugs. Some kind of sedative, I don't recall." He frowned a bit. "I don't like it."

He'd lost his usual iron grip on his feelings, thoughts, and expressions, and my heart broke a little for him. Of course, I'd always wanted him to relax more, but not under these circumstances.

Because …

My heart skipped a beat as the realization sunk in.

I cared about this man lying on the stiff hospital sheets. Against the odds, I cared about him. Maybe a lot.

As I grappled with my feelings, I fought to keep my voice from shaking. "I'm just relieved you're OK. Do the doctors know anything yet? Was it …" I didn't want to say it.

He exhaled slowly. "They don't think it was a heart attack, but we're waiting on tests. My blood pressure was very high."

I nodded. "I'm glad we don't have to ride in a helicopter tonight."

Something flashed in his heavy-lidded eyes as he gazed at me. "No, we don't."

Oh … I'd said *we*, but that was presumptuous. We'd only just started to become friends. I felt my cheeks color a bit and turned away briefly just as a different nurse knocked and entered.

"Hi there, Pete. How are you feeling?" he asked while setting up a few supplies on the bedside table. "I'm here to check your vitals. Can I have your right arm?"

"He prefers Peter," I said quietly.

The nurse glanced at me briefly before applying the blood pressure cuff. "Oh, did I say Pete?" He laughed. "Sorry, I did see a note about that, but it's been a long night."

I looked over at Peter, but his eyes were closed as if he was trying to block out everything.

When the cuff was removed, I gave him a small smile and touched his other arm lightly. "Well, I should probably go and let you rest … you look tired."

He opened his eyes and shook his head slightly. "Stay."

I felt a pang in my chest that I didn't care to examine. "Oh, um, are you sure? You look very sleepy."

"Stay for a bit," he said just before turning back to the nurse.

"Well, your vitals are definitely much better than they were when we admitted you. We won't have results on the tests until morning though. You should rest for at least a few hours."

When he didn't respond, the nurse winked at me. "Don't be stubborn, Mr. Auclair. Your girlfriend can stay for a bit to make sure you fall asleep."

My eyes widened as they met his and then darted to the nurse, who was packing up to go. Before I could correct him, the nurse waved a hand. "Have a good night, both of you. The night nurse will check on you next time, as I'll be heading out."

Peter merely nodded a couple times before his eyes fluttered as he tried to focus on me. "Stay?" he mumbled.

I nodded, my worried eyes wandering over his very still body as I reminded myself it wasn't a lifeless body but just a relaxed one. An exhausted one. I pulled a chair closer and placed my hand over one of his. He squeezed my hand but only with minimal strength.

I squeezed back and then bit my lip. I wasn't his girlfriend, and I had no business pretending to be. But if this man needed me to stay, then I'd stay.

Chapter 17

I woke to a beeping sound, light chatter, and an achy back. My eyes found the clock on the opposite wall, and I squinted and then blinked a few times. Nine-thirty?

I guess I'd eventually fallen asleep in the chair by his bed, but I must not have slept very long, as I recall seeing the clock hit 6:30 am before I'd slept a wink. I'd played on my phone for a while until my battery eventually died. Mari and Terry had texted back around midnight, and I assured them I'd stay and keep an eye on things.

It made me feel slightly less weird to have a real purpose for being here, other than just ... wanting to stay close. Because I did.

I lifted my neck off my shoulder carefully, wincing at the inevitable pain and stiffness. My eyes landed on Peter, still lying on the hospital bed but reading a newspaper now. "You're awake," I said, my voice sounding like a frog.

His eyes were immediately on mine, and I gazed into their depths. His eyes—his whole face and posture—seemed much more alert but somehow different than usual. It felt like his eyes were penetrating mine somehow, trying to communicate something without words ...

I yawned, scolding myself for imagining things. If he was trying to communicate anything, it was probably surprise or gratitude. Nothing terribly deep. Or maybe it was just some lingering effects of the benzodiazepine they'd given him. I sipped from the water bottle I'd left on the ledge by the wall and cleared my throat. "How are you feeling?"

"Fine." He set the newspaper aside, and his eyes never left mine, even as the nurse beside him started rattling off his stats.

"So, Mr. Auclair, these numbers are good. I think the doctor should be in soon," she said crisply.

"Is he going to be OK?" I heard myself asking in a slightly desperate voice.

"The doctor will be back to discuss the test results." This nurse was all business, not even offering a smile as she left.

I stood up to stretch my legs and walk around a bit before returning to his bedside. "Peter, I know you're a man of few words, but ... talk to me." I gave him an imploring look. "Your vitals look good, and thank goodness for that. But how are you *feeling*?"

He stared at me for a long time before his lips finally parted for a moment before speaking. "I'm not great with words."

My lips curved into a smile. "It's OK. I'm getting used to that, you know. How about I just assume you're feeling pretty good compared to last night ... you were really out of it. I was so worried, Peter. But now, you look almost like my usual grumpy neighbor." I laughed, hoping to convey I was teasing, a little.

"Your assumption is largely correct."

But the air felt tense between us, and I wasn't sure why. Deciding I should try to distract him a bit, I chatted for a while about the book I'd started reading on my phone during the night and even told him about the new phone game I started playing, even though I knew he couldn't care less.

"Those games always seemed like such a waste of time to me," he said.

I chuckled. "Yes. They are a waste of time, but sometimes wasting time is what you need to do. Does that make sense? After all, I had many hours to kill last night."

"Why?"

"Well, this chair wasn't really conducive to sleep, though I did eventually doze, I guess. Not that I'm complaining—I mean,

I'm not the one admitted—"

His eyes widened. "You spent the entire night?"

As I nodded, I wondered if that was presumptuous of me. "You may not remember, but last night, you asked me to stay—"

"I do remember. I just didn't expect you to stay the whole night."

My face flamed. He was right; he hadn't specified that. I just wouldn't have felt right slipping out while he was asleep, not knowing his prognosis and not knowing if he wanted me to stay. But now, in the cold light of day, it was clear I didn't have any right to stay the night. "Oh, sorry, I misunderstood," I said quietly, looking away.

He reached out and clutched my hand then, causing a warmth to shoot up my arm and straight to my heart. "Don't apologize."

When my eyes returned to him, I nearly gasped at the intensity in his eyes. He was grateful, I assumed; perhaps he'd never had a friend or even family member who cared enough to stay with him in the hospital. It was sad. And yet … I couldn't pin it down, but it wasn't sadness I saw in his eyes.

I had to ask.

It was probably the worst time—if there was ever a good time—but I needed to know.

I gently let go of his hand and breathed in and out slowly. "Um, I did have a question. Why didn't you tell the nurse last night that I'm not your girlfriend?" I heard my voice shake a bit and hoped he didn't notice.

He shrugged, and his face held the usual stoic expression. "Why would I?"

My voice was incredulous. "Uh, because I'm not?" That was a good reason, wasn't it?

His warm gaze swept over my face slowly. "Well, what are you then?"

I inhaled sharply. Oh my—what was he implying?

Wiping my sweaty hands on my pants, I swallowed with serious effort. "I'm your friend, Peter."

His stoic expression *still* didn't change as he uttered the words I never expected to hear. "I think we both know you're more than a friend, Hazel."

My jaw dropped, and then my lips began to quiver.

Did he mean—

I had to have heard him wrong. Or misunderstood … but what else could it mean?

Maybe he meant we were not just friends but *best* friends. But that didn't seem likely either. We'd only known each other a few weeks and … something about his face told me that wasn't his meaning.

"Wha–what about Valentine's Day?" I stammered. "You … you hated that we spent it together. Stormed out of my house, even."

I knew it was a massive risk to bring this up, but I'd been unable to forget about the perplexing incident, especially considering the passionate kiss we'd shared just before that.

He sighed and looked at the wall for a long moment, so long I was convinced he wouldn't reply. "I've always hated the holiday."

I felt my encouraging smile wobble. Whether I was dating or not, I was a romantic. And hearing this admission from him hurt my heart.

But this wasn't about me.

After a moment where he seemed to consider whether to continue or how much to say, he swallowed slowly and then spoke, "My parents loathed each other. Father put all his energy into the business, and what little time he had left, if any, was for his affairs. And there were many. On the rare occasions we saw him, he was verbally abusive to both of us. I began to feel grateful when he was gone on business trips, or so he called them, because the atmosphere between them became so toxic."

I merely nodded, sadness and empathy coursing through me as I studied this grown man in front of me who'd endured this. I gripped his hand and saw some of the tension leave his face.

"So, it was just my mother and me most of the time, and I learned to be OK with that. And Fluffy and Furry." He glanced over at me and rolled his eyes. "If it's not obvious, I named our pets."

Offering a small smile, I said, "I love it."

"Anyway, we were close when I was little, but she eventually became more distant. I guess she was breaking down herself, I don't know, but I was a little boy so I couldn't have understood that.

"One morning when I was ten, I woke up to find my mother gone, along with Fluffy. She'd written a brief note that I don't remember very clearly, and the housekeeper consoled me until my father got home late that night. He was of course no help. Instead of comforting the boy whose mother had just abandoned him, he seemed to resent me more than ever. I could never please him after that, though I rarely had before it either." He took a few steadying breaths before finishing. "And that day she left ... it was Valentine's Day."

I gasped. "No."

As he nodded, the pain etched into his features was evident. I'd never seen him so open about his feelings. If only I could hug him, but climbing on top of him in his hospital bed might be frowned upon.

"I assumed the date was intentional to send a message to my father. But now, as an adult, I don't know. Maybe the holiday just made her finally give up on any chance of romance with him. She must have had her reasons."

I shook my head. "No. No! Don't rationalize this. No matter what her reasons were, she didn't just leave your dad. She left *you* too. That's ... inexcusable. Did she at least call you? Visit?" My parents had at least waited until I was eighteen before splitting up. My little sister hadn't been so lucky though.

His exhale was shaky as he shook his head. "Not for a long time. A couple years or so."

My eyes filled with tears, and I looked away, not wanting him to see me crying—because this was about him, not me. I tried to discreetly wipe my eyes before turning back to him. "I'm so sorry, Peter. I don't blame you at all for hating Valentine's Day." My mind raced. "Oh, so that's what set you off—"

"Yes," he said with a grimace. "She *had* called me on the holiday, and I deleted the voicemail without listening to it. And when she brought it up so casually last night … I just lost it, I guess." He studied me then. "Tell me something. She didn't come to the hospital, did she?"

I couldn't lie. Shaking my head sadly, I squeezed his hand. "I'm sorry. I was shocked, to say the least, when she claimed she had to get back to the hotel."

He shook his head, looking down. "You know, it's fine—"

"It's not fine!" I exclaimed.

"I've had a long time to accept this," he reminded me. "I never expect anything from her. Or him, for that matter. He was disgusted with me when I quit the business recently, which isn't surprising."

I wrinkled my nose in distaste. "It's not? I would think a father would be concerned first and foremost about his only son's health."

He let out a chuckle. "One would think that. But not him. He never approved of anything I did, even though the business was far more successful after I took over years ago, when his health forced him to retire. For similar reasons, actually. I don't know what his deal was, but he's always seemed disappointed with me. Either that or … irritated that I exist."

My eyebrows scrunched together as I processed this. "I'm so sorry, Peter. How awful." My heart was breaking for that little boy, but also for the man who sat next to me and shrugged, even though he was obviously struggling with his feelings.

"Like I said, I came to terms with all this years ago. Or at least I thought I did." His lips curved downward.

"It makes sense. By showing up here, she opened up the old wounds. And that was before she even mentioned the date of her Valentine's call so flippantly." I searched for the right words to say but came up empty. "I get it, you know. I was already eighteen when my mother left, but it was still traumatic. I still remember every detail about the day before she left, when I burned some food and she looked so disappointed … silly now that I think about it. But anytime I burn something in the kitchen, the memories assault me, and I can barely breathe." I squeezed my eyes shut, trying to block out the memory. "I get it, kind of. It doesn't make it any easier. But I'm sorry, Peter."

He lifted a shoulder then. "She's gone. Got a text from her about an hour ago, something about Randall needing her." His exhalation was shaky.

"But *you* needed her too," I said, my voice nearly a whisper as I squeezed his clammy hand.

He squeezed it back and then reclined against the single pillow on the bed. I stared at his weary face; Peter was nothing like I'd imagined. The real Peter, inside. When he let his guard down.

And he thought we were more than just friends? Or had I misinterpreted that?

Suddenly, I needed to know. Now.

Perhaps I should wait until he's out of the hospital.

But …

"Peter," I found myself saying as he looked at the ceiling. But as he swung his head toward me, a knock sounded at the door, and I stood.

"Hi, Peter? I'm Dr. Bakshi. How are you feeling this morning?"

"Fine," he said curtly. When the doctor seemed to be waiting for him to say more, he added gruffly, "Impatient."

The doctor grinned. "That's what we like to hear." Then he looked at me with a wink. "No, but really, how is he?"

I smiled back at him. "His usual insufferable self. In other words, pretty good."

Dr. Bakshi sat down on the chair I'd left empty. "I have the results of your tests."

"Should I wait outside?" I asked, biting my lip because I wanted to stay but not to intrude.

The doctor merely looked at Peter, who said, "No."

"Very well. None of the tests showed any sign of a heart attack or other serious condition. Your blood pressure was extremely high, but that's not atypical for your condition."

Peter's brow was deeply furrowed as his eyes shifted to me and then back to the doctor. "I don't understand."

"You had a panic attack," said the doctor, his lips curving upward slightly. "That, combined with your hypertension and arrhythmia, probably made it seem worse than it actually was."

Peter's eyes were huge as I waited for him to respond. "It was all in my head?"

"Well, no, the symptoms were very real. But also very temporary and not indicative of any health concern. At least not a physical health concern." The doctor hesitated a moment. "Some patients meet with a counselor though. If you're interested, I can put in a referral."

Peter said nothing but stared at the ceiling for a long time as the doctor and I communicated silently.

"I have even better news. You can go home shortly. I'll just send a nurse with the discharge paperwork."

At this news, Peter perked up and sat up straight before swinging his legs off the bed. "Thank you."

"You're welcome." For a moment, it looked as though the doctor might say more, but he merely said, "Have a nice day!"

I found myself smiling as I turned to look at Peter, who was stretching his legs as discreetly as he could with a hospital gown on. When he caught me staring, my cheeks reddened. "Oh, sorry. I'll wait outside so you can change."

"Wait, Hazel?" he called out.

My gaze held his for a moment. Surely he wouldn't ask me to stay while he—

"Thank you." His lips twisted into a small but genuine smile.

My heart did a little flip, and I did what any sane woman would do.

I pivoted on my heel and promptly tripped.

Well, maybe not so sane.

*****

The ride home was quiet, and while I didn't sense any tension from *him*, I was feeling all sorts of uncertain. We still had a lot to talk about, didn't we? Some of the things he'd said … well, did he mean them? And if so, what then?

After arriving home, he walked me over to my house. Who'd have thought this guy who was initially so abrasive was actually a real gentleman?

We stood a foot apart on my front porch, and he took both my hands. "Hazel, thank you."

I smiled while shaking my head. "You have nothing to thank me for."

"You were there." He squeezed my hands before letting them go. "Thank you."

Impulsively, I leaned forward and threw my arms around him. His response was hesitant at first before he wrapped his arms around me. Tight.

And I realized I hadn't felt this good in a long time.

Maybe ever.

I stepped back, my lip quivering. "Bye, Peter. Get some rest, OK?"

He stared at me and then nodded. "You too. We'll skip our walk today, right?" He smiled faintly. "Goodbye, Hazel."

When he didn't move to leave, I figured he was waiting for me, so I did one of the hardest things I'd done in a long time. I turned and, with a little wave, left him on the porch.

Inside, with the door closed, I stood immobile for a long, long moment.

When I finally became aware of my surroundings, I swiped at my damp eyes and cheek, kicked off my boots, and resisted the urge to go look out a window facing his house. After padding to the bedroom, I threw back the covers and sank into the bed.

I wasn't really tired. I just needed ... maybe the comfort that a cozy bed and blanket offered. Or maybe I should sleep. The oblivion of sleep would be welcome. At least better than this weird mix of sadness and confusion that clung to me.

Not long after I got comfortable in my cocoon of bedding, not caring that I'd worn these clothes for over 24 hours, my phone buzzed. I groaned, realizing it was still in my sweatshirt pocket. I considered not answering, but what if it was Peter? Maybe he needed help.

Or something else.

I peered at the phone, which indicated that Jeff was calling.

"Hello?" I said in a muffled voice.

"Hey, it's Jeff. Is this a good time?" he said in his usual rapid, crisp voice.

I cleared my throat. "Uh, sure. What's up?"

"I have news about your future business," he said with only a brief pause. "We have a potential investor already."

I almost dropped the phone. "*What?* Seriously?"

"I wouldn't joke about this," he said sternly. "There's a catch though. It's an angel investor, and they want to remain anonymous."

My tired brain took a moment to process this. "What? Why would anyone want to do that?"

"It's not that uncommon. Investors may do it for a variety of reasons. For example, maybe they don't want to attract attention to their business or be seen as open to funding other ventures." He paused. "Sometimes it's more personal reasons. It varies."

That was strange to me, but ...

"*What?*" I shrieked. "Someone wants to invest in my new idea—in *me*? Jeff, I love you today!"

"Glad to hear it," he said dryly.

"Seriously, this is ... amazing. When you said 'anonymous,' do you mean the investor just doesn't want their identity public? I'll still know at least, right?"

"In this case, no. That's one of the terms of the deal."

I gasped. "Oh. Well … what if I wanted to thank them?" I bit my lip. "I suppose I should just be grateful. I mean, I *am* grateful. *So* grateful. I—" I stopped when hearing Jeff's throat clearing. "Sorry, I'm just so—so astounded. Happy."

"Right. So, I'm booked up tomorrow, but I was thinking we could meet in a few days to go over all the terms in detail."

I nodded even though he couldn't see me. "That sounds good. Have Roxy set it up?"

Jeff was silent for a beat before responding, "Does she need to be involved?"

"She's my assistant, Jeff. And she's really committed to this project."

He sighed. "Fine. I'll be in touch. Congratulations." Then he ended the call.

My head dropped back onto the cushy foam pillow, and I grinned at the ceiling like an idiot. This news was amazing. Unexpected, so soon. But amazing.

I wondered if I should text Peter, and my grin slipped. I should let him get some rest and do … whatever he does all day. I'll call him later.

And wasn't it a little odd that he was the first person I thought to share the news with? I should really call Mari first.

For now, I just wanted to hug my body pillow for the next million hours. I wasn't that tired now, but even when not sleeping, my bed was by far the most comfortable place in the universe.

I really wasn't that tired though.

Chapter 18

Turns out I was tired. No, exhausted. I'd slept until late evening and then rose to grab a snack and check my phone. With no messages from Peter, I'd crawled back into my sleepy haven.

Now, it was well after sunrise, and I was baking chocolate caramel banana muffins. I'd just taken them out of the oven when the doorbell rang.

My heart skipped a beat. Who could it be this early?

With my apron still on, I ambled over to the door and opened it, but no one stood there. I looked around until my eyes traveled downward, landing on a large red box.

It was heart-shaped.

My heart jumped into my throat, and I looked around again, still seeing no one, even in the direction of Peter's house.

Peter … could it be him?

This definitely didn't seem like the work of Peter.

But who the heck else would give me a heart-shaped box?

I picked up the box and went inside. Just as I was about to open it, I stilled. It could be Mari. I'd texted her last night while snacking to let her know I was exhausted but Peter was fine. She might have sent them to cheer me up, since I hadn't yet told her about the investor news.

I opened the box, finding chocolates and deciding to sample one. But I barely tasted it as I chewed absently. For some reason, a pang of *something* was lodged deep in my chest. Disappointment? But that didn't make sense. It was wonderful

172

to get a gift from a friend. The very best friend.

But something gnawed at me as I mindlessly set the box on the counter and started lifting the muffins out of the pan.

You wanted it to be him.

I shook my head, refusing to admit this to myself, but then I sighed. I *did* want it to be him. So much.

You know why.

My heart lurched, and I froze.

You're falling in love with him.

I gripped the kitchen counter, stunned by the force of this realization. My breathing was erratic as the undeniable feelings swept over me.

When the doorbell rang again, I gasped before nearly running to the door.

But on the front porch was a teenage girl holding a large bouquet of roses in nearly every color. I stared at the flowers and then at her. "For me?" I said, my voice sounding high pitched.

She nodded with her eyebrows raised, the unspoken message being *Yes, you idiot. Why else would I be standing here?*

I didn't see any card in the bouquet. "Who are they from?" I called out as she started to leave.

She grinned. "Must be a secret admirer."

Inside, I'd begun cleaning up the kitchen when the doorbell rang yet again. This time, a bouquet of red and pink balloons was tied to my porch railing.

And for the next two hours, I answered the door every fifteen minutes or so to find a new delivery, each more beautiful and romantic than the last but none containing the sender's name.

By late morning, I was a mess.

Looking in the bathroom mirror, I scanned over my pink, tear-streaked face and unwashed hair. I'd taken off my apron, but my pajamas underneath still bore the marks of messy baking on my sleeves and chest. I was an absolute mess.

And I'd never looked more beautiful. Because I saw, there in the mirror, a sparkle in my own eyes that I'd never seen before.

A slight upward curve in the corners of my lips that seemed stuck there. As if I had all the reason in the world to be …

Happy.

Full of joy at the possibility …

Well, it was a possibility, technically. But there's no way that anyone else could've sent these deliveries. Not Mari, not anyone else I knew.

Only one person.

"Why are you wasting time staring at yourself in the mirror then?" I asked aloud before dashing out of the bathroom and to the front hall, where I stuffed my fuzzy sock-clad feet into boots and thrust my arms into my heavy coat. I threw on a hat too, since it was snowing. Because of course it was snowing again.

The few seconds before Peter answered the door seemed like an eternity.

He opened it slowly, taking in the sight of me. He didn't look surprised to see me. "Hello, Hazel."

The way he said my name … I might have swooned. But instead I gripped the edge of the doorframe firmly. "Are you going to let me in?"

He stepped back, amusement in his eyes. "By all means." When I stepped inside and then started to remove my damp hat, his thumb found my mouth. Stunned, I gazed up at him.

"You have something here … looks like chocolate," he mumbled as he gently dabbed at the left corner of my lip, while I held my breath.

I swallowed with great effort and then stepped out of my boots and threw off my coat. "Peter, what's going on?"

He stood with his arms crossed. "Pardon?"

I bit back a smile. "Playing coy doesn't suit you."

His eyes widened a bit, growing more intense.

"Then again, maybe it does."

And then I went for it.

I stepped forward, gripped his shoulders, and planted one firm kiss on his warm lips before gently biting his lower lip and then releasing him. As I took a step backward, I asked with a straight face, "Now will you tell me what's going on?"

His eyes were shining. "We're redoing Valentine's Day. I want *this* to be my new memory. Our new memory." He took my hands with such tenderness that I almost teared up again. "I want to be with you, Hazel. I want *us*."

I smiled through the inevitable barrage of tears welling up in my eyes. "It just so happens I want the same thing. You probably already know that by now. But I have to ask you something."

He squeezed my hands lightly. "What is it?"

Taking a deep breath, I examined his face closely for a reaction as I asked, "Did you invest in my new company?"

He pursed his lips. "What if I did?"

"I can't let you do that," I said, feeling grateful, relieved, happy … but it was too much. I couldn't ask him to do this. Could I? Then again, I hadn't asked. He'd just gone and done it.

A shadow of doubt passed over his features. "Why not?"

"It could fail."

He smiled then, and I was undone. I forced myself to look at his eyes, full of intensity as he replied, "You could never fail. And I need something to do anyway. I can't think of anything better to do with my money than investing in your business. In *you*."

I smiled back at him. I couldn't say no … I didn't want to.

Somewhat shyly, he added, "Can I be your part-time finance guy? Or number cruncher? I already offered myself up as a financial advisor to Terry and Mari, but they declined since they've already got some guy named Jeff."

I pretended to think about this for a while. "What about the animal shelter?"

"It's only a few hours a week. And my regular cardiologist agreed I could work if the hours are reasonable and the stress relatively low. I can't be a CEO anymore, but I—I don't think I want to anyway." He stepped closer to me. "Please give me a job and put me out of my misery. And … will you be my Valentine?"

Instead of answering him, I pulled him forward, grasping the sleeves of his shirt as our lips met. "Only if you'll be mine," I whispered against his lips before we both laughed.

"Done," he agreed, pulling me closer. "Happy Valentine's Day, Hazel."

Epilogue

"**S**o, I know you don't like being called Pete, but what about Petey? Petrov? Or—"

"No nicknames," he said with a gruff smile as he whirled me around the dance floor.

At least some things never change. Well, I couldn't exactly say he was still my grumpy neighbor, as I'd moved into his massive house just before Christmas. Neighbors no more. My grumpy boyfriend, then. But I couldn't even say *that* anymore either.

Because he was now my grumpy fiancé. He'd asked me to marry him last night, and I was giddy with excitement trying to keep it a secret until midnight, when we'd decided to announce to everyone.

Because it was New Year's Eve and I was turning thirty, and it just felt like the right time. Everything about him felt right, and I couldn't believe I'd wasted years of my life doing anything *but* being with this man. I was over-the-top madly in love with him. And judging by the way his eyes devoured me tonight, I knew he adored me too.

"I can't help but think back to a year ago. Remember when we met? You were so rude."

"Hey, I was not—"

"Come on, you were terrible."

The corners of his mouth curved upward slightly. "Fine, I wasn't the friendliest. But I was trying to keep my distance. I had to."

I frowned. "Why?"

"I knew you were dangerous."

I raised an eyebrow. "Dangerous? Me?"

"Yeah, you. You unsettled me. I knew I could fall for you." He paused, spinning me around. "And it was terrifying."

I smiled. "So, instead of letting yourself bask in the glory of all things Hazel, you chose to keep me at a distance by being a total jerk?"

He made a face. "Well, when you put it like that—maybe I was an idiot."

"Oh, you definitely were," I said, standing on my tiptoes to kiss him. "But so was I. I spent weeks trying to forget about that maddening guy I met at a wedding on Christmas Eve. Months, actually."

"Well, that was your first mistake."

I smiled wryly. "Was it, though? It brought you to me, didn't it?"

"And here we are. Dancing on New Year's Eve."

"I thought you didn't dance."

"I don't. Ever."

He whirled me around then, and I laughed. "You could've fooled me. You've been hiding these mad dance skills all this time! I should be mad at you."

"But you're not. Happy birthday, Hazel," he said, pulling me closer. "I do believe I'm even looking forward to Valentine's Day next year. That'll be a first." And then he smiled. That smile … it caused me to miss a step, only narrowly avoiding stomping on his feet.

As I righted myself, a couple caught my eye off to the side. I squinted, unable to believe what I was seeing.

"What is it?" Peter asked with a frown when I gasped.

I closed my mouth and then opened it again. "It's Roxy. Dancing. With Jeff."

His eyebrows rose. "I thought they didn't get along."

"They don't. And that's putting it mildly. But they look …"

Peter changed directions so he could covertly see what I'd been describing. "Cozy. Flirting, maybe."

"Yes! She's gazing up at him like … and is that an actual grin on his face? I didn't know he was capable of that." I shook my head in disbelief.

"Love can change a man," Peter said softly, leaning in close.

I smiled at him. "Yes, but ... surely not Jeff. They are the farthest thing from in love. Maybe they're just celebrating the fact that my new counseling center is finally open, so they won't have to meet regularly anymore."

After a silent moment, he started steering me farther from Roxy and Jeff and closer to the seating area. I looked up at him in question, and his lips were pressed together as though he was uncomfortable. And then he smiled, but not at me.

I turned to see who he was gracing with his smile and—

Peter held my arm as I nearly tripped on my heels upon seeing the familiar faces.

The two people who'd watched me take my first breath.

My jaw was surely on the floor as I stared at them and then glanced at Peter with wide eyes. Soon we were in front of them, and I leaped into Dad's arms and then pulled Mom in for the group hug.

"Honey, it's so nice to see you. Happy birthday!" my mother said, her eyes shimmering with tears.

"Mom, Dad—how are you *here*?" I asked as I stepped back but just a bit. I grabbed Peter's hand and pulled him closer. "Peter, did *you* arrange this?"

"He did," Dad said. "He called a few weeks ago."

My eyes widened even further. "You called my parents? But why?"

"To ask for your hand in marriage, of course," he said, as though that were such a normal thing to say. "And to invite them to visit for your thirtieth birthday."

Tears were pooling in my eyes as well as I smiled and threw my arms around Peter. "I can't believe you did this. And ..." I turned to my parents with a more serious expression. "And you came."

"Of course we came, honey," my mother said, pulling me closer. "We love you."

Dad nodded. "We want to visit more often. This is your home now. You even run a business now. I couldn't be more proud."

Mom stepped back. "In the past, honey, we figured it was easier for you to visit us, since you had such a busy schedule. But now that you're settling down, that's all changing."

I smiled through more tears. I always thought … well, I thought I wasn't important to them. Not worth coming back to the States to visit. And all this time … they'd hesitated only because of my busy schedule?

Peter knew me so well. "They were thrilled to be invited, Hazel."

I nodded, unable to believe what I was hearing, full of emotion that was hard to contain.

"Peter, I can't thank you enough. Are you ready to tell everyone our news?"

He stared into my eyes, and I now knew that was just how he communicated. He was quiet with his feelings, and that was OK. I smiled and wrapped my arms around him again for a long hug. When I heard my parents clearing their throats, I pulled back reluctantly and laughed.

Something caught my attention out of the corner of my eye though. Someone was literally stomping off the dance floor … it was Roxy. She had a murderous expression, and Jeff was following from a few feet behind, not looking too happy himself.

I nudged Peter and tilted my head in their direction. "I guess their truce didn't last long."

Peter just smiled and shook his head, giving them only a brief glance before finding my eyes again. And he didn't need to speak, because in his eyes I saw everything. All the love I was feeling too, and more, so much more. I wiped a tear from my eyelid and smiled. "I love you, Petey."

He rolled his eyes, and one corner of his mouth lifted. "Fine, I'll allow it. Just for tonight. Because tonight we're celebrating you."

"No," I said, squeezing his hands. "We're celebrating *us*."

BONUS! Get Peter's perspective and find out the exact moment when Peter realizes he's head over heels in love with his feisty neighbor.

This bonus chapter is available here for free when you join my newsletter:

https://dl.bookfunnel.com/lbveajzc3m

Acknowledgments

When Mr. Highbury suggested—only a week after releasing my first novel around Thanksgiving—that I write a sequel to *Meet Me on Christmas Eve* and publish it on Valentine's Day, I laughed hysterically. My exact words were "Yeah, no." Yet the seed had been planted, and I couldn't stop thinking about Hazel's story. By December, I had committed to this crazy idea and started penning my fourth novel. I knew that keeping up with my writing goals over the holidays would be tough, but I underestimated just how challenging it would be. As always, my ideas are far bigger than my ability to execute them all. Still, I kept at it, and I wrote a love story for Hazel, a fan favorite from my first book. I hope you love Hazel and Peter's story as much as I do.

I have to thank my support team, who came through for me once again. The all-star team includes my cover designer, Stefanie Fontecha of Beetiful Designs; my PR advisor, Amanda Kerr; and my web designer, Emily Rusu. I'm also grateful to the reviewers, editors, and other bookish people who've supported me; there are far too many to list, but I appreciate each and every one of you.

Readers, I can't thank you enough, but I'm always going to try. My absolute favorite thing about publishing is being able to connect with readers. I *love* hearing from readers, so don't hesitate to reach out anytime. The romance reader groups online are some of the best groups of people I've ever encountered, and the writer groups are amazing as well.

Finally, I have to thank all my friends and family for the overwhelming support and praise for my first book. I never expected so many of you to read my novel, and I'm humbled and thankful that so many have. Last but not least, I'm overflowing with love and appreciation for Mr. Highbury and our children, who inspire me every day and who try their best to be patient while their mother juggles her day job and hours of late-night writing.

A Humble Request

Thank you for taking the time to read and review! Even short reviews mean so much to independent authors.

If you loved this book, please consider leaving a review or rating:

- *Amazon*

- *Goodreads*

- *BookBub*

If you didn't like the book but want to offer feedback, feel free to email me at ***alana@alanahighbury.com***. I'd like to hear more about what didn't work for you. Whether it's something I can fix or just not a fit, I'd be glad to hear from you!

Readers, you are my favorite kind of people. Thank you.

About the Author

Alana Highbury is the author of the holiday romances *Meet Me on Christmas Eve*, *Snowed In on Valentine's Day*, and *Dance with Me on New Year's Eve*. She's also written a trio of Jane Austen-inspired novels releasing in 2025. Her novels blend rom-com, contemporary romance, and women's fiction. When she's not writing, you can often find her reading, playing board games, cross stitching, or hanging out with her family, which includes a writerly husband and children, two beautiful, lazy cats, and a feisty cockatiel.

With a master's and bachelor's degrees in English, Alana has worked in professional writing and editing roles for two decades, but she's been an avid fan of romance fiction even longer.

Visit her website at https://alanahighbury.com, and follow her on social media and bookish sites:
https://www.facebook.com/alanahighbury.author
https://www.instagram.com/alanahighbury_author/
https://www.goodreads.com/alanahighbury
https://amazon.com/author/alanahighbury
https://www.bookbub.com/authors/alana-highbury

Books In This Series

Love & Holidays

Meet Me On Christmas Eve

A second-chance romance set at Christmas in a snowy small town

Snowed In On Valentine's Day

An enemies-to-lovers romance with two neighbors stranded together in a snowstorm

Dance With Me On New Year's Eve

An enemies-to-lovers, secret-identity romance where our shy protagonist finds love and a fresh start